When the Storm God Rides

Tejas and Other Indian Legends

By

Florence Stratton

First published in 1936

Published by Left of Brain Books

Copyright © 2023 Left of Brain Books

ISBN 978-1-397-67010-6

First Edition

PUBLISHER'S PREFACE

About the Book

"This is a collection of Native American lore from Texas. It is focused on the Tejas, a Caddoan group which called itself the Hasinai. The term 'Tejas' is from a Caddoan word which means 'friend,' and it gave us the name of Texas. The Tejas lived between the Sabine and Trinity rivers, in modern south-east Texas. They were the furthest west of the Southeastern native groups, in close contact with the Plains tribes, so their folklore reflects both regions.

Written in a simple declarative style to appeal to young readers, When the Storm God Rides is not a work of ethnology, but is based on genuine traditional folklore from the region. The material has been romanticized by the author, and sometimes softened for the audience, although not to the point of becoming maudlin as often occurs in this kind of book. However, since there is a paucity of material on the southeastern Native Americans, and specifically those from the Texas area, this fills a gap."

(Quote from sacred-texts.com)

CONTENTS

FOREWORD

THE Indian legends in this book have been collected by Mrs. Bruce Reid of Port Arthur, Texas, during forty years of travel over Texas as a naturalist. Mrs. Reid gathered these stories directly from full-blooded Indians or from persons who had Indian blood in their veins or from others long closely associated with Indians and familiar with stories recounted by their parents and grandparents.

A few of the legends probably have filtered in to the Tejas Indians from the ancient Mayan Indians of the Isthmus of Yucatan. "When the Storm God Rides" likely is of Mayan origin. The legend "How Sickness Came Into the World" was obtained by Mrs. Reid from the late Chief Sun Kee of the Alabama tribe in east Texas. "The Swift Blue One" undoubtedly is of Comanche origin, for it was the horse that gave Comanches their power. The bluebonnet legend, with that of the blanket flower, point also to a Comanche beginning.

From the late Jack Mitchell, a Texas hunter and a Texas ranger, a man familiar with stories known to a group of Texas Indian hunters long his close friends, the legends of the bluebonnet, the magnolia babies and many others were obtained. Jack Mitchell secured legends from his uncle, François Michel of New Orleans, one of that large company of French-Indian traders who often associated intimately with the aboriginals. Mitchell's wife and children are well known in southeast Texas, where they live. Mrs. Mitchell says that François Michel "sailed with Lafitte," and was related remotely to the noted buccaneer of the Louisiana-Texas coast. Although Michel's expeditions often took him well into the interior of Texas, the bulk of his trading in furs and hides was mainly done with the agricultural tribes west of the Sabine River. The trader's acquaintance with the Indian legends grew through his contacts with Indians in the course of trading in guns, knives, feathers, furs and trinkets. Campfire talks yielded many stories.

The most reliable guides in determining the origin of Indian legends are locale and subject matter. Legends of the Spanish moss and the iris, for instance, in all likelihood came from the Indians of east Texas, where this moss and this flower are most prolific. Different legends dealing with the same subject have sufficient similarity to show that they came from the same source; of such similarity are two bluebonnet stories, one involving the sacrifice of an Indian maiden of the Mexican tablelands and the other, which is included in this volume, dealing with a little Indian girl's sacrificing of her doll. The essential similarity of tales differing in details gives confidence to ethnologists investigating the folklore of the American Indian.

Some of these stories are known to be several hundred years old. Others are so old as to have their origins shrouded in the mists of time. The fact that in these legends is so seldom mentioned the horse, the forerunners of which became extinct in North America at a very early time, and which had to be introduced to the known tribes of Indians by the white man, is strong evidence of the antiquity of the stories.

The anonymous authorship of nearly all old folklore is characteristic of Indian legends. Although collected in Texas it is certain that the legends include material from the Southwest as a whole and have undergone alterations from time to time while passing from one tribe to another and also through breed and purely white sources. Indians were in general a roving people; the discovery in Louisiana and Texas of artifacts of obsidian and copper, materials not native to the region, exemplifies this well-known fact. It is but natural that not only the weapons and implements but also the cultures of different groups and different periods should become rather widely dispersed.

The illustrations, by Berniece Burrough, are combinations of authentic Indian symbols, and are the result of careful research.

FLORENCE STRATTON.

WHEN THE STORM GOD RIDES

THE shores of Texas along the Gulf of Mexico did not always have islands along them. The Indians who lived a long time ago on the coast have left behind them the story of a god and his great black-winged thunder bird which he rode like a horse over the Gulf at certain times. He was the Storm God, and he made islands where none had been before. These islands were made as homes for the wild birds, the sea gulls, the big pelicans, the cranes and the herons.

The god of storms did not live among the Indians, but lived down in the warm seas below the Gulf of Mexico. And for this the Indians were glad, for his terrible thunder bird, named Hurakan, filled the people with fear. The tribes which lived near the Gulf only saw the mighty god when he rode his thunder bird through the skies. He visited their land when he wanted to get the white and colored feathers of birds living on the seashore for his cloak. The Indians could tell when he was on the way. As Hurakan, the thunder bird, came swiftly through the air over the gulf, the sky in front of him became filled with bits of white clouds sailing high over the beaches. Then the wind began to blow, first here, then there. At last came the great thunder bird in the shape of a cloud which closed the eye of the sun and made the land dark. Then the wind grew strong and howled and blew as the god and his thunder bird came flying through the sky. The Indians ran into their wigwams and held them down as best they could while the Storm God rushed by and snatched feathers from birds to put on his cloak. The Indians were happy when he was gone because Hurakan made them afraid. Even today Hurakan comes back once in a while in the shape of a storm which people call a hurricane.

There was a day when the peaceful tribes who fished in the Gulf were driven away from their homes by fierce tribes from the north. Unlike the Indians who lived on the coast these tribes liked to kill. When they saw the birds flying around, they shot them with arrows. They caught them on their roosts at night. They robbed their nests. The poor birds cried out at the tops of their voices for the Storm God to save them.

Far off down in his home in the warm seas the god lifted his head and heard their cries. Quickly he rose to his feet and shook himself. Thunder broke loose over his head, so angry was he. He ran and jumped upon the back of Hurakan. He shouted for Hurakan to hurry. Shooting fire like lightning from his eyes and shaking loose black clouds from the tips of his great wings the Storm God's thunder bird flew toward the Texas coast. He and the god were wrapped in darkness, and as they flew across the sky the day became like night and the waters of the Gulf broke into white foam.

The Indians who were killing the birds saw the thunder god coming too late to get away. The sun was gone and the clouds were so thick that the day was like night. The wind from Hurakan's wings hit the Indians and blew them down when they tried to run. Behind them came the waters of the Gulf, pushed upon the land by the wind stirred up by the Storm God's thunder bird. The wind ` blew the birds high in the air, but it drove the water into the camps of the bad Indians and scattered their homes and made the Indians climb into trees. The Gulf now poured far inland over the prairie, and the prairie was like the sea. Everywhere was rolling water, leaping waves, crying winds. High above the earth the Storm God rode his thunder bird and shouted with joy while the wind blew his long hair loose through the flying clouds.

At last the god went away. As he left, the waters of the Gulf began to roll back from the land, and when they reached the ocean bed again they dropped the mud and sand they had torn loose from the land and brought with them. The mud and sand began to pile up. Soon many islands were forming. They rose higher and higher as the waters kept dropping their loads of earth around them. When all was done the Texas coast was dotted with islands that were new homes for the birds. Indians could not reach those birds any longer. The pelicans, the gulls, the sand pipers and all the others now went to their new homes and made their nests where they could be safe and where the Storm God could find them when he wanted new feathers for his cloak.

To this day those islands remain. Dwarf trees, cactus plants, weeds, grasses and flowers cover them like fairy gardens. And thousands of birds live on them, sing amid the bushes and bathe in the little pools left by the rains. During spring and summer they lay their eggs and raise their little ones. They are happy and safe from men, because long ago the Storm God built the islands for them.

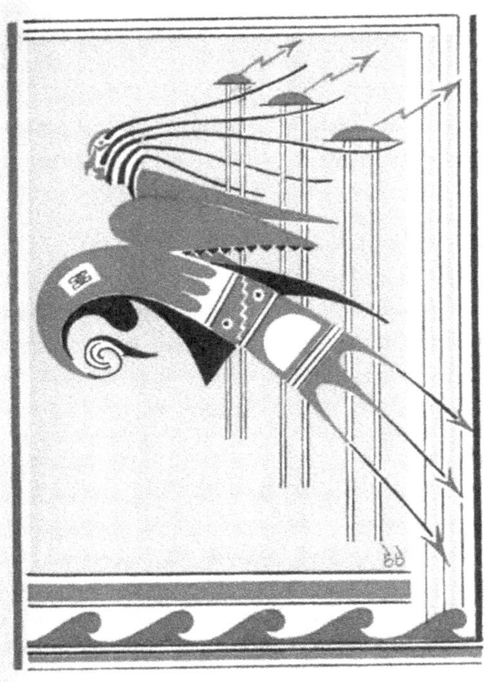

HOW THE NORTH WIND LOST HIS HAIR

THE howling old north wind is afraid to come to the country around the Gulf of Mexico. Only now and then does this cold fellow dare to come into the south, and when he does he does not stay long. He is afraid of the strong young south wind. Once the two winds had a great fight. There are still signs of that fight in the southern woods. The Natchez and the Tejas Indians, who lived along the Gulf, had a story to tell about the north and the south winds and why the moss that grows in the trees is a sign of their fight.

The two winds hated each other. The north wind was a strong, fierce old man with long, thick, gray hair. When he came into the southern woods, where the south wind lived, he would rush around blowing cold out of his mouth. His gray hair would fly behind him like a dark cloud. Nobody liked the old north wind. The Indians shivered in their tents and the flowers closed up and died when he came around. But everybody liked the warm young south wind, for he lived there. The flowers always opened up when he touched them with his soft hands and breathed upon their buds. The Indians would roam through the woods when he was with them.

From time to time the north wind and the south wind would grow angry with each other. The old north wind would come down out of his country where he belonged and try to drive the south wind away from his home along the Gulf. Sometimes he would bring his blanket of snow with him and stay for weeks. When the south wind would try to drive him out of the woods and send him home again the north wind would puff up his red cheeks and blow cold air around, and his long gray hair would fly over his head.

One spring the old north wind came south and would not go away. He stayed for many weeks after the flowers should have been coming out and the birds should have been building their nests. It was so cold the leaves would not come out on the bare limbs of the trees. June came, but still the Gulf country looked as it looked during the winter months. The north wind kept blowing the south wind out over the Gulf, and because of this the spring weather would not come.

Finally the young south wind became tired of staying over the Gulf so long. He made up his mind to gather all his power and to enter into a great fight with the north wind that had driven him from his home. Filling his lungs with all the air he could hold, the south wind rushed across the water toward the land. He hit the north wind a mighty blow. When the two winds locked themselves in each other's arms and began howling in each other's faces the Indians ran into their tents, thinking the Storm God was riding over their heads on his thunder bird that breathed out the lightning. The fighting winds knocked around the clouds in the sky and tore them to pieces as they fought. They pulled up trees; they caused great waves to dash on the beach, they whirled birds around in the air, they tore up the snow that lay on the ground. They ran through the trees, they rolled on the earth and they clawed and shrieked.

At last the young south wind began to get the better of the old north wind. The old fellow was out of breath, and because he was out of breath he lost his power. Then the south wind wrapped his arms in the north wind's long gray hair and began whirling him round and round over his head. He whirled him faster and faster. A strange thing happened. Part of the north wind's gray hair broke loose, and he flew howling through the air.

There stood the young south wind with his strong arms full of hair. He was so happy that he began dancing around and swinging the north wind's hair over the trees. The birds sang and the Indians shouted, for they were glad the south wind had come home again. As the south wind danced and whirled around he let the hair loose, and it fell all over the trees, and where it fell it took root. There it grew and it still grows today. It is called Spanish moss. It hangs from the magnolia, oak, gum, and other trees in long, gray beards that sometimes dip in the streams.

The north wind does not stay in the south any more. When he sees the moss he remembers that fight with the south wind and he leaves as fast as he can.

KACHINA BRINGS THE SPRING

AN Indian tribe living in the south-western country was once filled with fear and suffering. It was the beginning of spring, when the green buds should have been peeping from the trees, and new flowers should have been lifting their fresh, cheery faces from the grass, but something was wrong with this springtime. It was not like spring. There was no rain from the hard blue skies that looked down without tears of pity on the hills and prairies that would not flower and the dry creek beds where water used to flow. And the weather should have been warm, but it was bitter cold. In the day the sun was far away and had no heat. In the night the moon and stars were like cold steel in the wide, black sky, where no clouds floated.

And because of these things the Indians suffered great hunger. There was little food, only parched corn and acorns and shreds of dried buffalo meat. Gone were the wild deer, flown away were the wild turkeys, gone were the buffaloes. The animals and the birds which the Indians used to shoot and eat could not live there without water and food, and they had died or had left the country. And the berries that the tribe needed to eat could not grow in the dry, hard earth. There was no rain to call them up from their sleep under the ground.

The Indians wandered over the hills in search of food, but they could find none, and they began to starve, the skin on their bodies became loose, their bones began to show through their flesh. Their women and children grew weak and moaned or cried in the night because they were hungry.

One night the tribe's medicine man, the wrinkled, wise old Indian who warded off the evil spirits and who knew how to get the good spirits to grant the Indians' wishes, came out of his wigwam and beat loudly on his drum. He was calling the tribe to come to listen to him. The Indians hurried around him and watched him in fear as he pounded on his drum and danced and shouted a song. The starving dogs, when they saw his painted face and his red eyes burning with the light of the camp fires, howled and ran away with their tails between their legs and hid. They knew there was a strange power working in him.

Suddenly the medicine man cried to the Indians, "Ho! Hear me! The Great Spirit has thundered in my ears and told me to speak. He has taken away from us the rain and the flowers and the animals because we have angered him. But he will give us help if we will make him a burnt offering. We must burn something which we love most and gather its ashes and scatter them to the four winds of heaven. Then the winds will carry the ashes to the Great Spirit and he will be pleased again. Go back to your wigwams and think what we love most. Tomorrow we will burn it when the sun rises."

Among the Indians who listened to the medicine man was a little girl. She was holding in her thin arms a wonderful kachina doll made for her by her grandmother. This kachina was far prettier than any of the others in the tribe. It was made of wood carved with a flint knife. Painted on the wooden form were the clothes of a warrior, an Indian brave. On its head was a war bonnet of blue feathers and its eyes were made of two little black beads dyed from berries. The little Indian maiden loved her kachina, carried it with her when she played and slept with it in her arms at night.

When this little girl heard what the Great Spirit wanted she almost cried, for she felt in her heart that nothing among her people was more loved than her own doll. But she looked up and saw the shadows of pain in the face of her hungry mother. She saw how thin was the face of her baby brother strapped to his mother's back in his cradle. She remembered low moans in the wigwams at night, and she knew her people suffered because the Great Spirit was angry. She looked down at her beloved little doll, held it tightly to her breast and slipped away to her father's wigwam where she lay for long time with her face pressed close against her doll.

The lodges were still and the fire in the middle of the camp had died down to red embers when the little girl came out again. In her arms was her doll. She knew she loved her kachina more than anything else was loved in the tribe, and she had decided to give it up as the Great Spirit had asked, so that her people would be happy again. She cried a little bit as she laid twigs on the dying embers of the fire. But she blew the fire until it sprang up into a blaze that made the shiny eyes of her doll sparkle, so they seemed to be bright with tears, like her own. She hugged the doll and kissed it. Now she laid it in the middle of the flames. Quickly the flames began to eat the doll. The blue feathers on its head were gone, the tiny shoes turned into smoke, the beady eyes fell off the burning face into the fire, and soon there was nothing left of the doll the little girl had loved.

Now she raked out the ashes and sat down to watch them cool. When they had cooled she took them in her two hands and held them up while the cool wind blew them out of her hands and into the darkness. Finally the little girl stooped and patted the ground where the ashes of her doll had lain. Then a wonderful thing happened. Where the ground was bare and hard before, it was now covered with soft leaves that felt warm to her cold little hands. The sharp cold of the night wind now was gone, and the smell of spring flowers seemed to fill the air around her. The Great Spirit must have been pleased with the offering of her doll. Happy once more, the little girl hurried to her wigwam and lay down to sleep.

In the morning the child was awakened with the sound of joyous cries outside. She heard drums beating and heard dancing feet. The Indians were singing. She peeped outside and saw that she had pleased the Great Spirit, because for the first time in many moons a misty rain was falling, a rain that was good to the thirsty earth. The cold wind was gone, too. The warm south wind was gently blowing through the rain and rustling trees that were heavy with new green leaves.

She went outside and saw a wonderful sight on the hills around the camp. Everywhere the hills and prairies were covered with strange and lovely flowers the Indians had never seen before. When she ran to pick one of them she saw that they were shaped like the little bonnet of feathers her doll had worn, and blue like those feathers. At the heart of each small blossom was a speck of red, just like the red of the fire which had burned her doll. And the tips of buds were silver gray, like the ashes that were left after it had been burned.

When the little girl hurried with one of the new flowers to the Indians they knew what had happened. She had given her doll to the Great Spirit and he had given back to her millions of flowers that were now lying on the hills like a piece of blue sky fallen to earth. And spring had come at last. The Indians named the new flowers bluebonnets, because they were like the blue bonnet of the little girl's doll. Today, when the bluebonnets appear on the Texas prairies, it is a sign that the Great Spirit has once more returned springtime to the earth.

THE SWEET GUM'S AMBER TEARS

THERE was no finer looking tree in the forests than the sweet gum in the days before the sweet gum knew what it was to cry. High and straight in the woods it rose. Its leaves were like stars of shining green. Its green seed balls, covered with tiny spikes to keep the seeds away from birds, swung on their stems as the wind blew. Birds liked to build their nests among the sweet gum's branches in spring. These things made the tree proud. It lifted its green head as high as it could, and it reached higher toward the sky than all the other trees.

There was one thing the sweet gum did not understand. The redbirds never built their nests in its boughs. One day a redbird came to the tree and the sweet gum asked why it never built a nest there. "Why do you never stay long when you light on my boughs?" asked the tall tree.

The redbird answered, "I like to sit among your branches and look over the country, but you grow too tall, like the pine tree. Those who dwell in the sky do not want things on earth to come too close to them. They send down the lightning to keep the things of earth away from the clouds. Lightning strikes the pine tree, and one of these days it might strike you."

It happened at last just as the wise redbird had said. A storm came up one day. The lightning lashed its forked tongues across the sky and with a loud crash it struck into the top of the tall sweet gum. Ever since then the children of the sweet gum tree have been weeping clear amber tears down their trunks, because they fear that when they are grown and their heads are over those of the other trees the lightning will strike them too. It often happens that way.

THE PLANT THAT GROWS IN TREES

THE mistletoe is a strange little plant. It does not live on the ground with other plants, but always is found growing up in the limbs of trees by itself. Only the birds can reach the little white berries which appear both in summer and winter. That is why the mistletoe plant is found only in trees. And a bird once put it there because it had pity on the mistletoe.

There was a time when the mistletoe plant did grow on the ground as a small bushy plant. One day when it was growing on the ground a bird called by Indians the thunder bird, which they thought caused the thunder, lit on the mistletoe. The thunder bird was hungry because it could find no berries on other plants. But it found berries on the mistletoe and began to eat them. At last, when the bird had eaten all it wanted of the little waxy white berries, it thanked the bush.

"I am glad you liked my berries," said the mistletoe. "I shall not be here long because I shall soon die." Its leaves were drooping as if it were very tired.

The thunder bird opened its red beak and asked, "Why must you die, little plant?"

"Because I am green the year around," said the mistletoe. "My berries grow in winter when the other berries are gone. Many animals feed on me. They break off my brittle branches when they chew me. I shall not live long."

Then the thunder bird took pity on the mistletoe because the bird had liked the little berries. "I shall take you from the ground and put you where the animals that walk on the earth cannot find you any more," said the bird.

The thunder bird took the plant in its strong beak and flew up to the top of a mesquite tree. It fastened the roots of the mistletoe into the fork of a limb. Then the bird flew down to the ground and brought back some earth on its beak and packed the earth around the roots of the plant.

"Now, little Mistletoe," said the bird, "you will grow up here in this tree, and the animals will not get your berries."

"Yes, I will grow but when I die my seeds will fall to the ground and they will suffer as I did," said the mistletoe.

The thunder bird laughed and answered: "Oh, but I will see to that." The bird then wiped his long bill, to which stuck some of the berries of the mistletoe, on a limb. "See?" saic the bird. "The berries stick on the limb. They will grow there, like you. And whenever other birds eat your berries they will wipe their bills as I do and the seeds of the mistletoe will continue to grow forever and ever."

And that is why the mistletoe keeps growing in the trees.

WHY THE WOODPECKER PECKS

THEN you hear a Tap! Tap! Tap! sounding in the top of a dead tree or at the top of a telephone pole in the spring time you look up and what do you see? A woodpecker, of course! No bird but the woodpecker and his kinfolks pound on dead wood with their beaks.

You look up at the woodpecker and there he is, looking just like a little man in a black coat and a red hat. And he is smart. If he sees you looking at him he stops pecking and slips around the other side of the limb or the pole and only sticks out his red head to peep at you.

There was a time when woodpeckers used to be Indians.

A certain plant that grew on the desert was called the mescal plant. Little knobs or buttons which grew on this plant had, when eaten, a magic power. The Indians who ate them had visions or dreams. They could see their gods and talk with their ancestors. But only those Indians who were medicine men and had the right to see strange things had the right to eat the mescal buttons. They warned everybody else not to touch them, or bad luck would come to them.

One man did not listen to the medicine men. He wanted to know what the medicine men saw in their dreams when they ate the mescal buttons and then fell down to the ground or wandered about the camps singing with their eyes closed.

This Indian boy slipped out one night away from his people, when the wolves were howling far off on the desert, and went to where the mescal plants were growing. By the light of the bright stars he could see the buttons growing on the plants. Half afraid, he picked one. Then he put it into his mouth. Because it tasted good he picked more and he ate them. It was not long before everything was strange before his eyes, and the desert seemed to grow bright with light and to be filled with moving things that looked like the gods the medicine men talked about. The boy was thrilled. When he tried to walk towards the gods he fell down and wonderful colors seemed to swim in the air around him as he lay on the ground. Then he fell asleep.

The next day the boy whispered to other boys what had happened to him when he ate the mescal buttons. They were tempted by what he told them. That night they slipped out of the camp with him and ate the buttons and they saw the strange visions that he had seen on the desert. Then these boys began to tell their fathers about it. The fathers ate the buttons and they told their wives what they had seen. It was not long until all the Indians of the tribe were eating them. They laughed when the medicine man told them that trouble would come. They stopped hunting, stopped weaving their blankets, stopped planting food, stopped gathering berries. All they did was to eat the mescal buttons and to roll on the ground while they had strange visions.

The mothers and fathers forgot about their poor little children. At last the children became so hungry that they began to wander around looking for food. They wandered from the camp and began looking among the bushes and trees and stones for something to eat.

After all the children had gone one young mother who had not eaten many of the mescal buttons opened her eyes. When she saw that her child had gone she looked quickly around the camp and could not see any of the children at all. She then jumped to her feet and started crying out. She beat the other Indians until they too awoke. Then they all began crying for their children, but they could not find them.

What had happened to the children of the tribe? The Manitou, one of the gods that make the clouds in the sky and hurl the lightning, had found them hungry and hunting for food, and the Manitou had taken pity on them. He had hidden them all away inside of hollow trees, where they would be out of the hot sun and safe from the wolves.

The Manitou, when he saw the Indians looking for their children, appeared before them and told them what he had done.

"Oh, what can we do to get them back again?" cried the weeping Indians to the Manitou.

"I will turn you into birds, and you can go look for them in the hollow trees. When you find them I will turn you all back into people again," the Manitou said.

He waved his hand over the Indians. They became birds. The black robes they were wearing turned into black feathers, and the red feathers they wore in their hair turned into the red head of the woodpeckers. Then the tribe flew off to the trees and began tapping every tree with their sharp bills to find their children.

Even yet the woodpeckers tap the trees. When they find bugs they eat them because they are hungry, but they keep on tapping to find their children.

THE WOODPECKER'S STUMPY TAIL

THE woodpecker, who knocks on the trees and cuts holes in them to find the bugs he eats, has a ragged, stumpy tail. He once had a long tail like other birds, but a fish bit part of it off.

It happened this way. Long ago a tribe of Indians lived in a country where floods often came in the spring and covered the earth and bushes with water. One spring a big flood was coming and only the frogs knew it. One old frog had lived close to the Indians so long that he could talk some of their language, and this old frog climbed upon a stump near the village where the Indians lived and warned them.

"Run for your lives! Flood's a-coming! Run for your lives! Flood's a-coming!" he boomed with his deep voice as he squatted on the stump.

Nobody paid any attention to him. The old frog puffed out his chest and boomed louder than before, "Run for your lives! Flood's a-coming! Run for your lives! Flood's a-coming!"

Now the Indians heard him and laughed at the old fellow. A woodpecker was sitting in a tree over his head, and he also began to laugh at the old frog. The other birds did not laugh, but flew out of the low trees and bushes and went to trees high enough to be above the flood when it came. The woodpecker kept on laughing and stayed with the foolish Indians by the bank of the river.

That night the rain began to pour down from the black sky. The river rose and rose. At last it tumbled over its bank and began running through the bushes and into the Indian village. The thunder boomed. The lightning cracked open the clouds. As the Indians jumped from their beds and began climbing into the trees the rain poured from the sky in sheets and the flood began rising over the boughs of the trees and washing the Indians away.

Now the woodpecker was frightened. He could not see to fly at night, and all he could do was to flutter from tree to tree hoping to find one high enough to be above the water. He perched on the very highest limb he could find, but even then his long black tail was hanging in the water running under him. As he was clinging to the limb and wishing he had listened to the old frog, a fish saw him there and made a snap at his tail. The lower end of it came off in the fish's sharp teeth. That is why the wood-pecker has a short tail with jagged ends that look as if they had been bitten off.

CHIEF TWO HAWKS' TRAIL

A great hunter named Two Hawks stood on a dry, hot plain at the edge of his camp and looked far away across the dying bushes. Two Hawks was looking for signs of wild animals which the hungry Indians of his tribe could eat. But he could see none, he could see nothing but shining waves of heat, called sun devils, dancing over the desert. All the animals had gone because for many weeks there had been no rain in the land. Everything was dry, the creeks had dried up, the springs had dried up. Because there was no water the plants were dying, and because the plants were dying, the animals such as rabbits, the deer and the buffaloes, had fled away in search of food and water.

Day after day the sun burned in the hard blue sky. Now Two Hawks' tribe had become so weak from want of food that of all the men only Two Hawks himself, who was the strongest of them all, could walk around. The chief was looking across the land because he knew that he must soon leave the camp alone to see if he could find something for his people to eat. Far off he could see a mountain. He decided he would go toward that mountain to see what he could find.

Two Hawks was strong and brave, but as he walked over the burning ground where no grass grew he felt sick and weak. The sun beat upon his head and made him dizzy, but he walked mile after mile without stopping. Finally, after two days, Two Hawks came in sight of a deep canyon near the mountain. Tired and thirsty, the chief looked over the edge of the canyon. There, feeding on the grass that grew near the edge of a little stream at the bottom, was a herd of buffalo. Two Hawks' heart leaped with joy when he saw the animals. Although he was weak from hunger the Indian began creeping down the side of the canyon through the bushes. When he was close enough to the buffaloes he put an arrow to his bow, but he was so weak that he could hardly bend the bow. Finally he let the arrow fly. His aim was good, and one of the buffaloes kicked up a mighty cloud of dust and then fell to the ground.

Now there was food for the Indians! But when Two Hawks had skinned the dead buffalo and started to carry off some of the meat he found he did not have enough strength to carry it. What could he do? At last he decided to hide the meat in a little cave he saw in the side of the canyon. He would go back to the camp and return with some of the men.

As Two Hawks was putting the last of the meat into the cave, a large, fierce wolf which had smelled the meat rushed into the cave. Two Hawks did not see him, for he was bending over the meat. The wolf struck him on the back and sank his sharp teeth into the chief's neck.

With the last of his strength Two Hawks turned and began fighting the terrible animal with his bare hands. Finally he tore the wolf's teeth from his neck. As he did so the blood flowed out and streamed into his face, but Two Hawks did not care. He was going to kill this wolf. He seized the animal's neck in his still strong hands and choked it until the wolf lay still.

Two Hawks had won the battle. Yet when he got to his feet he almost fell down, for he had lost much blood. But nothing would stop him from getting back to his camp far over the plains. He must tell his people where they could find the meat. He staggered out of the cave and at last crawled back to the top of the canyon.

As Two Hawks went slowly back the deep cuts in his neck which the wolf had made still bled. The blood ran down his body and fell in drops to the hard, baked ground. As he went he became weaker and weaker. Finally he knew he was going to die before he could return to the Indians. He was glad that the drops of blood marked his trail, for he knew that if the Indians found his body they could follow the blood back to the cave where he had left the meat. But then Two Hawks saw that large red ants had begun to follow him and were eating the drops as fast as they fell.

When he saw this Two Hawks fell upon his knees and prayed to the Great Spirit to do something to keep the ants from eating the signs that marked his trail. He prayed for a long time under the hot sun, then got to his feet and tried to go on. When he had come close to the camp he fell to the earth and died.

The Great Spirit was proud of the chief's bravery. Because Two Hawks had done his best to help his people the Great Spirit leaned down from the sky and rolled a little ball of earth around each drop of blood, so that the big ants could not eat it. And so it happened that all along the trail of Two Hawks were little brown balls of earth. A party of Indians which had gone out to find their chief soon found his body. As they sadly picked him up they saw all around him the little balls. They saw them on the ground where the chief had walked. When the Indians broke open one of the balls they found the red blood inside, and then they knew that the Great Spirit had done this as a message to them. After they had taken the body of Two Hawks to camp they went back and followed the trail until they came to the cave and found the meat which Two Hawks had hidden for them.

When they brought the meat back to camp the Indians were so happy they wanted the spirit of Two Hawks to know how much they thanked him. They decided to gather the little balls and place them on his grave. But when they looked they could not find them. Something had happened to them.

It was not long after that until the rains came. When the dry earth had become moist once more, so that plants could grow in it, a new kind of bush appeared along the old trail of Two Hawks. It had small, thick, green leaves and sweet flowers that were purple-blue in color. As the flowers dried up the bush became covered with green pods that became hard, earth-colored balls, just like those little balls that covered the blood of Two Hawks. And inside each ball was a red seed, like the red blood of Two Hawks.

Today the seeds, which children make into bright red necklaces, are called frijolitos.

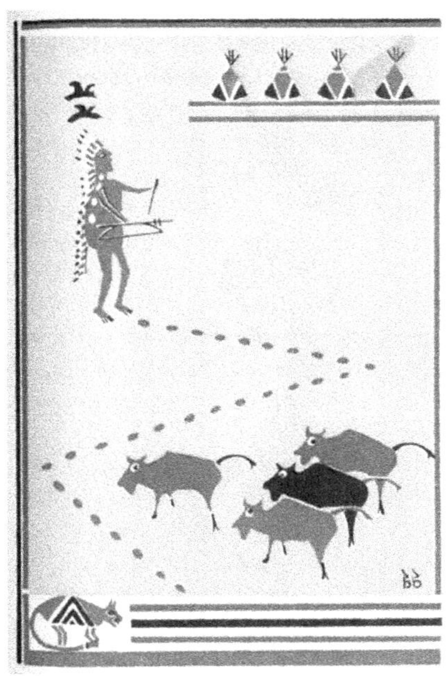

THE MAGNOLIA BABIES

LOOK into the heart of one of the large magnolia flowers that grow like white stars on trees in the woods. Inside is a little green-brown figure that looks just like a baby wrapped in his colored blanket. This is how the baby got in the magnolia.

Once some Indian babies were playing in the woods near a river. Across the river was a small bear, and he wanted to join in their fun. The babies saw him and waved their hands and laughed. The little bear stood up on his hind legs and waved his paws and growled. It was only a funny little growl but the Indian babies thought it was a big growl, and away they ran for the nearest tree, which was a magnolia tree. The baby bear thought they were running just for fun. Into the river he jumped. When he reached the other bank he growled again and ran after the little Indians.

Up the magnolia tree they climbed. Up climbed the little bear behind them, because he wanted to play. But the Indian babies didn't know this. Full of fear each one opened a bud of the magnolia flower and hid himself inside the white petals. And there they all stayed.

This is why the magnolia has the little green-brown figure of a baby wrapped in a blanket. He is wrapped so closely that you can't see his eyes, because he is still afraid a little bear is around.

OLD WOOLLY BIRD'S SACRIFICE

IN the forests the big flowers of the magnolia tree are like white stars scattered among the leaves. When warm days of spring come the broad white petals of the flowers unfold and fill the forests with sweet perfume. The magnolia is a fine, tall, evergreen tree. The story of its beginning on the earth is also the story of how an old Indian named Woolly Bird gave up his life for his people.

After a cold, windy spring in the days when the call of the wild turkey and the whoop of the Indian still sounded in the woods a drouth began. For almost a year a blazing sun, whose fires were cooled by no rain-filled cloud, baked the rich soil of the prairie country where an Indian village was standing. Hot days stretched into months. The prairie grasses shrivelled and died. Streams and ponds gazed into the fiery sun day after day until they dried up and left only their hard, dry beds to show where they had been. The earth was burned into powder which the hot winds blew into the sky in choking red clouds.

Drouth, thirst, and hunger came among the Indians of the village where old Woolly Bird lived. Though the hunters of the tribe kept to the trails from dawn to dark they found no game, for the deer and the turkey and the bear had fled from the nearby woods where the Indians hunted. Birds kept away from the waterless prairie. Roots had died in the earth, and the berries had failed to appear on their vines.

The Indians had to leave the prairie or die of starvation and thirst. They decided to leave their homes. As his people were making their plans to leave the village Woolly Bird, the oldest of them all, stood feebly leaning on his stick. His old heart was heavy with sadness. He was weak. He could do nothing for himself. While the other men and the women toiled, making ready for the journey that was to begin tomorrow, Woolly Bird could do nothing but tremble and murmur and stare through watery eyes, like an old grandmother.

They were preparing to take him along with them, Woolly Bird knew. They would share with him the little dried meat and the acorns they had left. The children and the women would have to give him food they need. When the tribe was ready to leave the next day they would put him with the weaker women and small children upon a drag made of young saplings pulled along by strong squaws. All this made old Woolly Bird full of sadness. He was useless to his people and he was eating their food and letting them take care of him. No Indian who had once been a strong man and a great hunter of buffalo liked to be a burden to his people in his old age. Death was better, Woolly Bird decided.

That night, when a dry blood-red moon was riding high above the hot prairie and gazing down upon the sleeping Indians, Woolly Bird rose from his bed and stole out of the village like a crippled ghost. He went as far as his feeble legs would take him and at last he fell down and dragged himself through the dust into the shadows of a dead thorn bush. The old man turned on his back and murmured his thanks to the Great Spirit. No more would Woolly Bird be a burden to his people. When tomorrow came, and they prepared to leave, there would be o crippled Woolly Bird to care for and feed, no whimpering Woolly Bird to be nursed like a papoose. Without him they would travel faster and their food would last longer. Woolly Bird turned his face to the moon and smiled with the pale smile of a man who has won a battle with himself. He was a man again.

But Woolly Bird's people did not leave him. When the next day came they found him gone from his bed, and they set out to look for him. Under the thorn bush on the prairie they found him at last, covered with dust and lying on his back, looking up at the sky.

"Come with us, Woolly Bird," said the chief, raising up the old man's head. "The tribe will not forsake its brave men. You have proved yourself brave. Get up and come back with us." They raised him and carried him back to the village.

It was not long after the prairie Indians reached their kinsmen who lived in the forests that the drouth blew its burning breath even upon the country that lay beneath the trees. Springs dried up. Creeks no longer ran in the dry beds. Fish and frogs buried themselves or died and turned to white bones on the hot, baked earth where the creeks and ponds had been. Birds flew from the dying trees, and there was no more food for the hungry Indians. Again they must pull up their wigwams and flee from the country which was turning to dust and ashes beneath the sun. Again must they find a new home, and this time, they decided, it would be along the Gulf coast, far from where they were. There was the great blue water, and its fish, and the white birds flying in the clouds that brought rain from the sea. Once more the Indians prepared to break camp.

As they worked to make the drags on which would be carried the weaker women and children and old people of the tribes Woolly Bird hobbled around to all the wigwams where lived old people like himself. With each of these old people he talked in a low voice, and what they talked about none of the others knew.

The Indians had fallen asleep the night before they were to begin their long journey to the gulf when from their wigwams silently crept the old grandfathers and grandmothers as Woolly Bird awakened them. Softly they took down their little white wigwams and folded them across their bent shoulders. With Woolly Bird they slipped out of the village. They made no sound but that of their tired breathing as they crept through the leafless bushes, over the dusty, dead grass and across the dry creek bottoms. For a long time these old Indians walked, with hardly a whisper among themselves. There was something they must do, and they could afford to waste none of their feeble strength in talk.

At last Woolly Bird led them down a steep hill and far into a grove of dead, rotting cypress trees whose bare limbs gleamed like bones in the faint starlight. Bravely they followed their leader as he pushed through thickets of brown, dry reeds and over fallen limbs. Now they had come to the center of the cypress grove.

"Here is where we stop," said Woolly Bird, dropping his wigwam at his feet. "Here is our camp, Old Ones Not Afraid to Die. Our people will never find us tomorrow. We will trouble them no more. Let us make our camp here. Here will the Great Spirit come to us and take us up to the sky to be once again with our fathers."

In the shadows of the lost place where no bird sang, no frog lived to grunt at the moon, and no living thing grew amid the dead reeds and the rotten limbs, the old people helped one another set up their little white wigwams. Then they lay down to wait. But the Great Spirit did not bring death to them. Because they were brave, and because they were willing to die to keep from troubling their tribesmen the Great Spirit loved them. He sent down to the still grove a great whirlwind. It ripped out the dead cypress trees as it roared through the grove, and in the holes where the trees had stood now sprang up tall living trees with silvery trunks and tops heavy with dark, shining leaves. And this whirlwind found the old Indians. It whirled their white wigwams about their bodies and then it lifted them in their wrappings high up among the boughs of the strange new trees.

There they remained. The Great Spirit turned them into the buds of a noble tree that is now called the magnolia. In the spring these buds open to form lovely flowers whose creamy white petals were the white wigwams of the old Indians, and whose brown centers were the Indians themselves. When the petals are ready to fall, bright red beads, laid there by the Great Spirit, appear around the necks of the brown centers of the flower. Then the beads drop to earth and there take root, for they are the seeds of the magnolia. The Great Spirit wants the tree always to live to tell the story of unselfishness.

A TRIBE THAT LEFT ITS SHOES

IF you will look at any one of our native orchids, of which we have about a dozen kinds, you will see that this flower has the shape of an Indian moccasin. Why do the orchids have this shape? It is because a long time ago they used to be the shoes of an Indian tribe.

In the early years of Indian history there was a large island somewhere out in the Gulf of Mexico. On this island lived a tribe of Indians. They were very wise, and because they were wise they made happy homes for themselves. They did not spend their time and throw away their lives fighting. Instead, they lived in peace, learned how to make fine vases, pots and bowls out of the red clay they found on the island. They built homes out of cane that grew around the edges of the island. And they liked to paint their clothes with the bright paints they made out of berries. They even painted their leather moccasins blue and yellow and red and white.

This tribe of Indians was happy until one night the top of the huge mountain that rose in the center of the island burst open with a loud noise and filled the sky with red flames. Great stones flew out of the hole on top of the mountain and rained down on the Indians' homes and gardens. Steam shot up from the mountain with the sound of thunder, and red hot, melted rock began running down the side of the mountain and burning everything it touched. Everywhere the Indians were rushing from their homes and crying in fear. Fathers lost their families. Mothers lost their children. Many of the people were hurt by the rocks thrown out of the thundering mountain. Soon the melted rock, called lava, began to flow into the village, and then the homes of the Indians burst into flames.

The chief of the tribe saw that they could stay on the island no longer, for everything was being burned. He led his people down to where they kept their canoes and ordered them to get in and paddle towards the nearest land, which is now the Gulf coast of Texas. It was a fortunate thing that the poor people left the island when they did. They were hardly a mile out in the water when all at once the whole island shook with a great noise which seemed to split the sky. Then with a roar the water surrounding the place where they had lived rushed over what was left of the island, and not a tree or a hill was seen any more. While the women and children of the homeless tribe wept in sorrow the men bent their strong backs and paddled towards the distant land somewhere in the mists that lay over the water.

A few days later the wandering tribe had pitched its camp on the beach from which they had been able to see their island far away. But they could see nothing now. The island was gone. All that remained of their homes were some bits of wood that floated onto the shore. The women began to weep. Then the medicine man of the tribe, who had been making wonderful medicine so that he could talk with the spirits, quieted them and told them that some day the island would come up out of the water again and they could go home.

But that would not be for a long time. The tribe had to move farther towards the north and away from the beach in order to find food, so the Indians broke camp, burned their canoes as an offering to the Great Spirit and began to wander away from the shore. As they passed out of sight of the Gulf they began leaving along the trail their painted moccasins so that they would know where to come to find their island again. The medicine man put a spell upon these moccasins to keep them from being moved, and he turned each one so that its toe pointed towards the spot where the island had been.

Months went by, then the years began to pass. Still the tribe kept going. The older people began to die. Soon the old chief began to fear that only the young Indians would be left and they would not know how to get back to the island when it was time for it to come up out of the gulf again. He went to the medicine man's wigwam and asked him what he should do. Without answering the wise old medicine man took the chief back on their trail to where the tribe had dropped the last painted moccasin.

Instead of the leather moccasin there grew in its place a little orchid, colored like the moccasin. And the part of the flower that looked like the toe of the moccasin was pointing in the direction of the island, which was south. They went farther along the trail and found more orchids, all colored like the moccasins and all pointing towards the island. Then the old chief was happy because he knew that his grandchildren of the tribe could still find their way back home.

If you go out in the woods and find an orchid growing on the edge of a swamp you will see the little flower pointing south. And you will know why.

THE CLOUD THAT WAS LOST

IN the country of high mountains the little white clouds that float around in the sky during the day go to sleep on the tops of the peaks. They do this because they become tired while waiting in the sky to grow heavy enough to send down the rains. All day the wind blows them this way and that, they bump into one another, and the sun makes them hot. Because of this they are glad when the sun at last goes down, for then they can float gently down to the mountain tops and curl themselves up among the trees and rest there until next morning. This is why people can see white clouds like fog on the mountains at night and at dawn.

Late one afternoon one little cloud had sailed off from its brothers and sisters. It had been chasing its tiny white tail like a puppy, had whirled and whirled head over heels until it was far away from the others. At last, when it was time to go to bed on the mountain tops, and all the other clouds were gone from the sky, the little cloud found itself all alone over a broad, flat land. It looked for the mountains but could not see them. The little cloud was lost. The sun was down and it was time to go to bed, but there were no mountains to be seen. A few drops of rain fell from the little lost cloud because it was crying.

After a while, just as the day was gone, the cloud was so sleepy it floated down and stretched itself out on the flat country, all by itself. Under it, where it was lying on the ground, were some sweet-scented, white flowers. These flowers were tired of being white. They had long hoped to find some way to color them-selves. Now the little sleeping cloud was colored light pink and lavender, and when the flowers felt the cloud float down upon them they opened their eyes and saw the lovely colors. They opened their throats and began to drink in the little cloud. They drank and they drank until at last the little cloud was all gone.

When morning came nothing was there but the flowers. Some were still white, but those which had drunk in the cloud were now pink and lavender, as the cloud had been. This is how the flowers called the wild phlox got their soft colors that look like the evening clouds.

THE SWIFT BLUE ONE

THERE was a time when the Indians had never seen a horse. When the first Spanish explorers brought horses with them in their ships to this country the Indians looked with great wonder upon the strangers as they rode, and thought that the horse and the man on its back were one animal. As time passed the Indians learned their mistake, but it was long before they were able to get some of the strange animals for themselves and to find out how to talk to them.

There was once a great blue horse that roamed the western plains. On his back were the tattered remains of what used to be a sky blue silken covering. The Indians of the country around never tried to catch him, but let him roam as he willed. To them this wild, free animal was a visitor from another land, from Spain, from a country which had sent powerful men in steel armor to them. Only one of the Indians had dared to ride the blue horse and he was the bravest of them all. When he died the Indians set the horse free, for there was fire in his eye and lightning in his hoofs.

This is the story of the great wild horse the Indians feared. A young Indian brave saw a Spanish warrior riding the horse through the hills. The Indian was afraid of this tall Spaniard wearing steel armor and riding the horse covered with silk trappings, but he rose from the grass and fired an arrow. The arrow struck the Spaniard through a crack in his armor and the man fell to the ground. His horse stopped and stood over him. Rushing from the grass the young Indian hurried toward the fallen man intending to shoot him again. The horse snorted and pawed the earth and the Indian became frightened and lowered his arrow. How was he to drive the angry horse away? He did not know. None of the Indians knew how to talk the horse language. He shouted. The horse only snorted again and bared his white teeth. The Indian backed away with a look of surprise on his face.

Seeing that the Indian did not know how to talk to the horse, the wounded

Spaniard made signs to tell him that if he would spare his life he would teach him the horse language. The Indian nodded and grunted. So it happened that the people of his tribe were surprised to see the young Indian riding into camp that day on the blue horse and holding the wounded Spaniard before him.

Over and over the Spaniard said the words which people use to horses to make them go or stop or run or walk, until the Indian learned how to speak them. At last the Spaniard died of his wound, but not before he had taught the Indian the horse language. Now the young brave was not afraid to ride the animal, but he was afraid to take from the horse the sky blue covering, because he thought it was a magic cloth needed to keep the horse from kicking the babies of the tribe and biting at the Indians' heads.

The great blue horse was fast as the wind. He could skim across the prairies like the cloud shadows, and his flying hoofs beat the ground like the roll of thunder in the summer sky. His master named him The Swift Blue One. The other Indians would not come near him. They did not know the horse language, and they were afraid he might dash them to the ground and slash them with his hoofs.

When at last the master of the horse was killed in battle the Indians decided they would get rid of him by turning him out on the prairie to roam away. They took him from the camp and turned him loose with the silk covering still on his back. And so it happened that for a long time a lonely blue horse roved across the country, sometimes running and stirring up the dust in clouds and always calling out for others of its own kind.

Finally other horses did come. They escaped from their Spanish owners and came to live with this lonely blue horse with the strips of silk covering flying from his back and neck. He became king of them all. The children of these Spanish horses became wild and ran in herds, and many of them were the children of the great blue horse from far away Spain.

THE WISE MAN'S BIG BALD HEAD

AN Indian tribe had in it a man who from his boyhood had always tried to find out secrets which nature kept from the Indians. He would not believe the old legends of his tribe. When he heard them he shook his head and walked away thinking. He did not believe many things his friends believed, and he believed things which they did not. This strange man said he wanted to know the truth about everything. He wandered from tribe to tribe asking questions. He looked long into the stars and wondered what made them twinkle and wink at him He kept thinking all his life, until he became known as a very wise man.

As this man grew older he lost his hair, and as he lost his hair his head seemed to grow larger. Finally, when he became an old man, he was entirely bald, and his head had become very large indeed. The other Indians said it was because his head was filled with so much wisdom that it had to swell to keep all the wisdom from running out his ears.

One day when the wise man lay sleeping the medicine man of the tribe looked down at him and thought what a pity it would be for all that wisdom to be buried with the man when the time came for him to die. The medicine man wondered about how it might be saved, for the old man did not have much longer to live. Finally the medicine man thought of something. He bent over and touched the old man's big round head with his long fingers and muttered magic words.

A strange thing happened. The wise man's body began to shrink as he slept, and his arms and legs began turning into stems and leaves. His big bald head took the shape of a squash growing on the stems and leaves. In this way the tribe never lost what was in the wise man's head, because the squash produced seeds which sprouted and gave them more squashes. When the seeds were dried and cracked they were very good to eat. They should have been, for once they were the wise man's thoughts and his great wisdom.

GRANDMOTHER RIVER'S TRICK

ONCE the little fish that lived in a river, who was their grandmother, were in danger of being eaten by the garfish. The garfish, because they were long and slim, could catch the little fish without trouble. When the little fish fled through the water and tried to hide near the edges of banks and in shallow places of the river the long garfish darted after them, poked their slim snouts into the hiding places of the small fish and snapped them up in their sharp teeth. The hungry garfish were everywhere. They ate and ate but were never filled. They swam after the little fish day and night, churned up the river mud and gave the little fish no rest.

The little ones at last cried out to their grandmother, who was the river, to do something to help them. Grandmother River did not like the garfish, and she liked the little perch, the bass and the minnows. She decided to play a trick on the big, hungry fish. She called to a big cloud that floated over her to send down some of its rain. The cloud heard. Twisting its dark, wet hair it sent down the rain in a great flood upon the river.

As the rain began pouring into Grandmother River she began to grow larger. She grew until she rose out of her banks and poured over the dry land. When the garfish saw what was happening they thought that here was a good chance to swim out upon the bushes and see if they could find something more they could eat. Instead of staying between the banks of the river with the little fish the garfish began to poke their noses into places where they had no business to be. They swam under the trees and the bushes and rolled their greedy eyes up at the grasshoppers and beetles.

And now Grandmother River played her trick. Quickly she gathered up her skirts to her knees and began running down to the sea, and as she ran she began dropping along her banks the dirt and sand she was carrying. Before the garfish saw what she was doing she had built up the banks higher than ever and had left them in little pools by themselves.

What a rage they were in when they saw how they had been fooled! They leaped in the air, they churned the pools, and they bit at one another. But it was no use. Grandmother River just gurgled along in her banks and the little fish played around as they pleased, happy to be safe from the sharp teeth and hungry mouths of the garfish.

WHY HUMMINGBIRDS DRINK ONLY DEW

HUMMINGBIRDS like to build their nests near water. The tiny little fellows like to skim over the surface of rivers and ponds and throw spray on themselves with the tips of their wings. They also like to flutter around in the first light drops of a rain. Yet hummingbirds do not drink the water in which they bathe. They sip nothing but the dew which sparkles on flowers and leaves. Why they are so careful about the water they drink is told in a legend.

Once a hummingbird and a great blue heron owned a lake together. It was a long lake which ran through the low country for many miles. Around the edges of this lake were moss-covered trees and low bushes which hung over the water. In the shade made by the trees and bushes the hummingbird liked to hover and drink the cool water.

Like many people the hummingbird and the heron had the bad habit of gambling. They liked to bet, and they bet about many things. One day the hummingbird bet the heron that he could fly from one end of their lake to the other faster than the heron. The one who lost the bet was to give up drinking in that lake and also in all others. Both birds agreed. They went to one end of the lake and started off together.

The hummingbird thought he would surely win the race, for he could fly much faster than the big heron, but he didn't know that he couldn't fly across the lake in one day. They flew on and on. The heron was left far behind, but still the hummingbird was a long way from the other end of the lake. Finally it began to get dark, and the hummingbird could not fly in the darkness. At last he had to fly to one side of the lake and spend the night in a tree, but the heron could fly at night, and he kept coming after the sun went down. The hummingbird didn't know it.

Early the next day the hummingbird jumped out of his tree and started on his way again. He expected to reach the end of the lake long before the heron, but when he got there he found the heron sitting in a cypress tree and laughing at him. By flying all night the heron had won the race. The hummingbird kept his word and never drank from that lake or any other lake or river again. That is why he sips nothing but dew today.

WHEN THE STARS TOOK ROOT

WHITE men teach that the moon is a dead, empty world. Yet there was a time, says an Indian legend, when a tribe of Indians lived and hunted there. The chief of that tribe had a lovely daughter who at one time visited the earth and who flung down from the sky, after she had returned to her father's home on the moon, a handful of bright little stars which took root and grew as flowers. She did this because she loved the son of a chief on the earth.

The tribe of Indians who lived on the moon never went into the narrow ring we see running around the moon when it is new. That was because the ring was a great forest without paths and filled with evil spirits. No Indian who had gone towards that forest of white, leafless trees ever came back to the tribe, and because of this the people knew that it was full of dangers.

The daughter of the chief of the moon tribe one day went close to this forest. She could do things which other daughters of the tribe could not do, because her father did not want her to marry and leave him, but allowed the young girl to do other things as she pleased. Thus it happened that the lonely daughter of the chief was wandering by herself when she came upon the edge of the great forest that looks like a silver rim on the edge of the new moon. Deep inside she saw a gleam of light that blinked like a dull red eye.

The daughter of the moon chief decided to enter the forest. After she had pushed through the white bushes, which made no sound at her touch, she at last came to a cave, and in front of this cave was burning a red fire. This was the light she had seen. Beside the fire, muttering to herself, was a strange old woman so old that only a few white hairs covered her head. Her nose was long and hooked, and it almost touched the point of her sharp chin. Her eyes burned like two coals of fire set deep in the tight skin of her face.

This old woman was bending over a blanket of many bright colors which lay at her feet. The daughter of the moon chief knew at once that this was a witch, for she had heard the medicine man of her father's tribe tell how witches looked. But the young girl was not afraid. She had been taught to respect old people. Instead of crying out in fear and running back through the silent forest she spoke to the old woman, calling her by the name of "revered grandmother" and asking whether she could do anything for her.

Being able to read minds, the old witch knew at once that the girl had only good will for her. She asked to be helped to the door of the cave. When the young girl had done this the witch invited her in to see some paintings which she had made on the walls. Without a trace of fear the chief's daughter entered with the toothless, stooped old woman, assisting her by the arm as they walked.

It was a strange sight which met the girl's eyes. All over the roof and the walls were painted signs in colors the girl had never seen before. The old witch read the surprise in the girl's mind and began telling her what each sign meant. The signs told of a far away place called the earth, how it looked and what kind of people lived there. Only a few of the moon's most powerful magicians, who had lived in the white forest, had visited the earth, she told the wondering girl. As she talked a strong desire to visit the earth came over the chief's daughter, and she asked the witch if this could be done.

Yes, it could be done, the old woman said, but only with danger. The girl did not care. She was willing to risk her life. The witch told her that only through a dark passage called "death" could she hope to return to the moon. But the young girl was not afraid.

At last the witch took up the bright blanket and wound it about the girl's shoulders, and as she did this the girl forgot all her life up to that moment. Now the witch drew from her robe an Indian flute made from a bone. She placed it to her dry lips and blew once, then again, then a third time. As the dying note of the flute was fading out in the depths of the cave the still air was suddenly filled with a rushing sound. With the speed of the wind a large eagle sailed into the cave, lit at the feet of the old woman and stood before her with his great wings still out-stretched.

This bird, which used to be an evil magician, was the witch's slave. With a wave of her flute she told the eagle to seize the young girl standing beside her in the blanket of sleep and to fly to the earth with her in his strong claws. The eagle obeyed. Out of the cave rushed the bird with the chief's daughter. Up above the white trees he rose, while his great wings roared as they beat the air. Soon they were far above the forest and flying as fast as the lightning towards the distant earth.

When the chief's daughter at last opened her eyes she was lying alone on the shores of an ocean. The eagle and the magic blanket were gone. But she was happy for she knew that she was now on earth. Rising to her feet the girl walked along the ocean listening to the strange sound of the waves and gazing at the flowers she had never seen before. It was not long before she came upon a camp of Indians near the shore. The people could not speak her language, but using the sign language with her fingers she told them that she had come from the moon and wanted to be friends with then. The Indians then took her to their chief. When he learned she was the daughter of a chief on the moon he gave her a fine wigwam of her own and took her into the tribe.

Not many weeks had passed before the chief's son fell in love with this lovely visitor from the moon. Because she fell in love with him they were married. All the tribe was happy, because the people liked them both. The women made the young man and his bride a large new wigwam painted all over with birds and animals and they made the bride some pots and bowls of clay so that she could cook for herself and her husband. The two young people made their home and were happy with each other.

Just before the next spring came the daughter of the moon chief had a dream. She had it the next night, and the next after that. She knew what it meant. She knew that the time had come, as the old witch had told her, for her to go back to her father's home on the moon. When the young wife told her husband he was full of sorrow, but then she told him that soon after her spirit had fled back to the moon he would follow her and they would live forever up in the sky with her father's people. And that made him glad again, and the two lay down together in their home and slept.

When morning came the moon chief's daughter did not open her eyes. Her hands were cold. Her husband bent over her and saw that life had slipped out of her during the night. He uttered a loud cry, for he knew that her dream had come true and that she was gone from him. Finally the people of the tribe came. The women wept and the men were sad and silent. At last they made her ready for burial. They carried her out. They laid her tenderly in the earth and placed beside her cooking pots and blankets for they thought she would need these on the moon.

That night the husband sat near her grave by himself.

The waves of the Gulf made the only sound that broke the stillness. Tired and full of sadness at being parted from his wife for a little while the young husband folded his arms and let his head sink upon them. Suddenly something made him raise his head and look up into the sky. He could see for an instant the misty shape of the one he loved, clad in the long robes in which she had been buried. She seemed to be made of the light that came from the stars. As he watched her she moved her hand and a shower of little stars began to fall towards him. Then he knew that the chief's daughter was on the way to her father on the moon and that she had thrown the stars down to him to let him know that she had not forgotten him.

Full of happiness the young man fell into a deep sleep and did not wake till morning had come to drive the stars from the sky. But morning had not driven them all away. All around his feet on the grass were hundreds of little flowers shaped like stars shining with the fresh dew. Some were white. Others were pink. Some had five pointed petals and some had six, but all had little hearts of gold. These were the stars that the daughter of the moon chief had thrown down to her husband as she left the earth.

Calling to the other Indians the young man pointed to the new flowers and told them how the stars fell during the night. Then they all knew that the girl's dream was true and that she would be waiting in the moon for the day when her husband would go up to live with her. Soon after that the young man was killed in battle. The people of his tribe laid him to rest by the side of his wife, and it was not long before the graves of both were covered with the little pink and white star flowers that can be found on the prairies today. The moon chief's daughter had thrown them down to tell the Indians that her husband had come up to her.

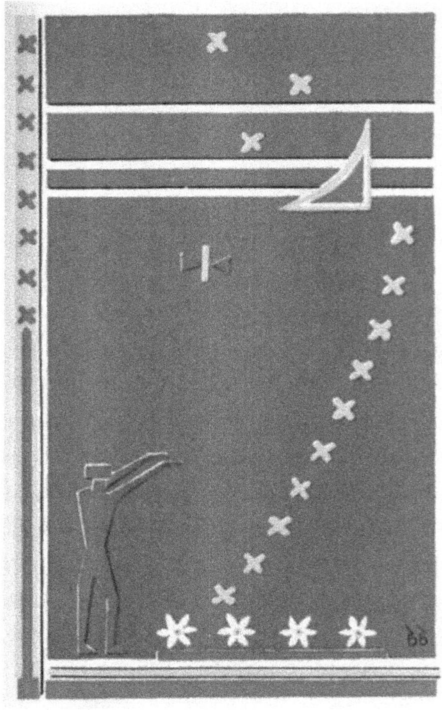

THE MAIDEN WHO LOVED A STAR

THERE was once a young and beautiful Indian girl who went from her home into a desert of the western country to gather there the purple ripe fruit of the prickly pear. She left the desert late one day after the sun had gone down, and when she set out for home the bright stars were beginning to sparkle in the sky. One star was much brighter than the others, and seemed closer to earth than the others. The Indian maiden stopped in the sand and watched it. Was the star winking down at her? She thought it was. She dreamed of the shining star that night, and she saw in her dream that the star was the home of a fine, tall youth, a sky dweller.

The next day the maiden went again into the desert to gather the fruit of the prickly pear. Again she stayed until the sun had gone down behind the distant hills on the far edge of the desert, and she watched her star winking once more at her. That was the sky youth, she knew. For seven days she visited the desert and each night she dreamed of this fair young man. She dreamed that he spoke of his love to her, but he could not join her on earth as long as she lived there and as long as he lived in the sky. He could not come down to the desert. She could not visit him in his star home.

The maiden was full of love, but she was unhappy because she was so far away from her lover in the star-frosted sky. She decided she did not want to live any longer. An old witch woman lived with the tribe, and the Indian maiden went to her and asked the woman how to die in order that she might be taken up to the sky to live in the star with her lover.

"Life is too great a gift to be flung aside," said the witch woman as she looked at the poor girl weeping on the other side of the old woman's fire. "You must live out the life the Great Spirit has given to you, but I can change you into a form that will permit you to live always out upon the desert under the loving smiles of the star youth."

Her words filled the maiden with joy. She went with the witch woman upon the desert that night. There the old woman made a powerful drink from desert plants and told the maiden to drink it. As soon as she had done so her feet began to take root in the dry, sandy soil. Her arms turned to branches. Her black hair turned to leaves, and the maiden had become a new shrub which no Indian had seen in the desert before. As the wind blew the shrub seemed to murmur thanks to the witch woman.

When the sky youth saw what had happened he leaned far out of an opening in his star lodge. He leaned so far out that the edges of the star broke with his weight, and he fell with sparkling pieces of star straight towards the maiden who had become a bush. The starry bits were shattered to fine dust that powdered the leaves of the bush with white. The youth was changed to purple blossoms. At last the maiden and the sky youth were together.

The bush with white-dusted leaves and beautiful blossoms became known as the cenisa, or ash-covered bush. Today it is called the purple sage. Not many white people know the story of how it came to the desert.

OLD QUANAH'S GIFT

WHY did old Quanah, the blanket weaver known among all the Indians of the southwest country, give so much time and care to a blanket which he had not finished after many years of work? The Indians of his tribe asked this question, but old Quanah always smiled and shook his head. Some day, he said, he would tell them.

Quanah, who had spent many years in the making of blankets, knew better than any other Indian how to put into them the beauty of color and form. He had once been a brave warrior, a fighter who took pride in his use of bow and arrow, and in following the trails of animals and enemies of the tribe. But when at last a poisoned arrow struck him in the leg and caused him to be crippled, he had to stay in camp and could no longer fight. Quanah, the proud fighter, did not like this. He did not like staying at home with the women of the tribe.

Because Quanah refused to be idle he at last began to make blankets, and because he was a man who took pride in his work he learned the art of making blankets with great care. Through forest and swamp he went seeking strange herbs, roots and flowers with which to make dyes that other blanket weavers had never used. He found out what were the best fleeces and fibers to use in making blankets smooth and warm and strong. He always made his own dyes with great care. He wove his blankets each time with different patterns, so that no two were alike. And he worked so carefully that he became known everywhere for his blankets.

Indian chiefs of other tribes heard of him and came to see him at work or to buy blankets from him. Other blanket makers came from many miles away to watch him make his dyes and weave the colored fleeces into his lovely designs. Quanah gladly tried to show them what he knew, but when they had gone away and tried to do as he had told them they found that they could not. They did not have Quanah's art, his magic touch.

For years Quanah worked. His blankets became famous. Some looked like the rosy clouds and mists of dawn. Others had the vivid colors of the red and yellow prairie flowers. Each one he made seemed to be better than the one before.

But there was one blanket which Quanah worked on year after year without finishing. Each day he would work a little bit on it, but slowly it grew until the Indians could see that in its center there would be a great golden, shining sun. Quanah was very careful in making the dyes for this blanket and weaving colors slowly into place. Around the bright sun other colors of sunset were woven. The red and purple of evening clouds were there, and also the yellow hues of thin clouds that were close to the golden sun. The Indians kept asking him what he was going to do with this wonderful blanket, but Quanah always smiled and said he would tell them when it was finished. Years went by. Quanah kept working, until he was so old that his fingers shook when he worked.

At last one day the Indians found the old blanket maker lying on a mat with his wrinkled face turned up to the skies. He was dying. But beside him lay the wonderful blanket, finished. Its many shades seemed to change as the Indians took it carefully in their fingers. The sun in its middle burned with the brightness of the real sun in the sky, and all the gleaming colors around it seemed to flow like the waters of the river when the changing lights of sunset struck them. As the Indians held this lovely blanket they looked down at old Quanah and saw that he was dying. Then they began to wail or to beat their breasts, because they knew they would never have another blanket maker like him.

But Quanah slowly opened his eyes and whispered to them: "My blanket is finished at last. Now I will tell you why I have made it with so much care and have put so much beauty into it. It is for the most worthy of our tribe. The man who has done most for his people is to have this blanket, so that our children may know that it is a fine thing for them to become good members of our tribe." And with this old Quanah's voice failed and he died.

Soon the Indians began to ask one another who should have the blanket. Who had done the most for his tribe? The chief called a council to decide the question. One man who was a brave warrior was pointed out as the right man. Another who was a great hunter of game was named. But the Indians could not agree about it. Some wanted this man; others wanted that one.

At length the chief held up his hand for silence. "We have forgotten the man who has really done most for us," said the chief pointing towards the still body of old Quanah lying before the tribal altar. "There he lies. Quanah himself should have the blanket. Is he not famous everywhere? Did he not make our tribe known far and wide?"

"Yes, Quanah must have the blanket!" cried the Indians. No longer did they argue. The old man who had made it was the very one who should have it, for he had done most for them. They did not like to see the lovely blanket laid away in the earth from all eyes, but they tenderly wrapped Quanah's body in its folds and then laid the old man and his finest work in the ground. Then each member of the tribe placed upon the new grave a large stone. At last they went away. They were sad because Quanah had died and because they could see the blanket no more.

But they were to see something as wonderful as the blanket. The spirit of Quanah, wishing them to have something of the beauty which they had buried with the blanket, gave its colors back to them in the form of a new kind of flower that began to grow among the stones on the grave. In these flowers were the same reds and yellows and browns which were woven into the blanket. There were the same hues of sunset in the flower petals. They were the same colors which white men later found in these flowers. White men now call them wild gaillardia, or blanket flowers, or fire wheels. Thus it happened that old Quanah gave a new flower to the world.

HOW SICKNESS ENTERED THE WORLD

SICKNESS did not always exist among men. It used to be that all Indians lived long lives and were never ailing until time came for them to die, as the time comes to all. Sickness was unknown in the world until two young Indians killed a messenger from the Great Spirit.

An old medicine man lay dying in his wigwam. He had been a great leader for his people, wiser than any medicine man had ever been before. He knew so many things that the Great Spirit decided to tell him how to leave his wisdom with his tribe before he died. The Great Spirit sent down word that he was sending a messenger who would meet him under a certain tree in the forest and tell what he should do.

But the medicine man became so weak that he could not get up to go into the forest to meet the messenger. He called two young men from the tribe. They should go to the tree, he told them, and hear what the messenger had to say and then they should come back to the wigwam and tell the medicine man. The young men went out and found the tree and sat down to wait. As they sat there a large snake came through the grass and raised its head to look at them. In great fear the young Indians took up sticks. They beat at the snake. When they had killed it they hung it across a limb and waited for the messenger, but nobody came. At last they went away and told the medicine man about seeing and killing the snake.

"You have killed the messenger of the Great Spirit!" cried the old Indian. "Some great trouble is to come to us, because the

Great Spirit will be angry." Then he fell back on his blanket and breathed no more.

Full of fright the young men decided they should bring back the dead snake and leave it before the wigwam of one of their enemies, so that the bad luck would come to him instead of to them. When the enemy came out of his wigwam and saw the dead snake he ran with it to another wigwam and left it there. Everybody in the camp did the same thing, for everybody was made fearful.

That night the mate of the snake came into the camp. She was very angry. At each wigwam where the dead snake had been laid she left an egg. By the time morning had come every egg had hatched out some kind of sickness, and so the first sickness was born into the world.

THE EVIL WATER SPIRITS

WHERE did the big and ugly fishes and the snakes that swim in the water come from? The Indians know. From their forefathers comes this story.

A long time ago, before the Great Father had finished putting all the kinds of fish into the rivers and shady streams, there was an Indian woman who was blessed with twins. This Indian woman was a very proud mother, for her two little brown, black-eyed babies were good to look at, and they had good tempers, and because of it other women of the tribe also wished they might have twin babies.

It was in the spring time, and the little twins were about four years old when they began to tire of staying in their mother's wigwam. Their mother, one day, had gone with the other women of the tribe to pick wild berries that grow in the woods and around the brier patches. Some of these berries the Indians ate as soon as they picked them, but others they dried and stored to eat in winter, when a blanket of frost covered the field and woods and few birds and beasts could be found.

The mother had left the little children with their grandmother. This old woman was wrinkled and weak, and sleep comes easily to such people whose eyes are made heavy and tired with the weight of many years of hard work and troubles. Lying down on a deer skin inside the wigwam the grandmother began to watch the twins as they played near at hand just outside the door. The day was warm.

Even the locusts in the tree tops sang lazy, sleepy songs, and the breeze that moved the leafy limbs of the trees whispered softly. The old grandmother began to nod. Her head sank upon her arm. Without knowing it she fell asleep in the wigwam.

When the twins saw their grandmother was asleep they put their heads together and whispered. Here was a fine chance to slip off and do something they had wanted to do for a long time. It was to do something that they had watched grown-up Indians do in the bayou that ran along the edge of the camp. The Indians waded in the bayou near its banks and bent down in the shallow water to dig up with their hands the tender roots of the plants called "Yonkupins" whose broad green leaves lift well above the surface of the bayou. These roots were good to eat. The little twins had seen the Indians gathering them and they wanted to gather them too.

Now their mother was away and their grandmother was asleep and they had a chance to do it. Without a word they slipped away from the wigwam when nobody was looking, and they ran without making a noise with their little buck-skin moccasins along a grassy path that led towards the bayou.

And now they were standing on the brink of a shallow place where a tongue of the bayou ran back into a low place in the banks. Everything was still among the high reeds that grew on the banks and leaned over the water. The twins looked down. They could see the bottom and weeds growing on it. What was in the weeds? They had been told by their mother that evil spirits were there, for she wanted to frighten them so they would not want to go near the bayou and be drowned. But they saw nothing, and they waded in, hand in hand.

They saw the broad green pads or leaves of lily plants floating a little way from the bank, and they knew that the roots were underneath, growing in the soft mud. Carefully they waded towards them. The water rose up to their knees. They were not afraid because they had not found the evil spirits their mother had told them about. They waded farther. The water was up to their waists. Now they were among the lily pads, and the long stems of the plants slipped against their brown bodies and tickled them. Here was the place to feel around in the bottom for the roots. The little boy and girl bent over and stretched their short arms down into the water around their feet. They had to bend until their chins were in the water and all their bodies but their heads were beneath the surface, but still they were not afraid, because even yet they had not seen the evil spirits their mother told them were there. It was so nice to be feeling with their fingers in the cool mud. The weeds growing on the bottom tickled their toes, and the leaves of the lily plants rubbed against their faces.

But just then, when everything seemed so easy and beautiful something happened. In pulling at a root one of the twins suddenly slipped and fell. Her head went under water. Then she became frightened, and with a scared cry she caught at her brother and pulled him down too. The evil spirits seemed to have them now. The lily stems wound around their bodies as they struggled. The warm water filled their open mouths as they tried to call their mother. They tried to get out of the clinging lily stems but they only slipped into deeper water and became wrapped tighter with the stems that were like ropes. They could not call for help for their mouths were filling with water. They could not get back to the bank for their heads were under water and they could not reach the bottom any more. The bright sun faded out swiftly, the songs of the birds were heard no more, the muddy water blinded their eyes and everything became dark. Poor little Indian twins! The evil water spirits they could not see had trapped them.

After a while the Indians came and found the children lying in each other's arms in the shallow water. They could not hear their poor mother wailing, nor could they hear their old grandmother moaning, and swinging to and fro in her sorrow. They could not see their father as he stood tall and still looking down at them on the bank while he sternly kept the grief of a father's heart from showing in a warrior's face.

That night, while the mother was sitting beside her twins for the last time, watching over their bodies before they were buried with their toys in the earth, she asked the Great Spirit to grant her a wish. For the sake of the other babies of the tribe she asked that the evil spirits of the water be given shapes that could be seen, so that the other babies would see them iii the water and be frightened away from them.

The Great Spirit granted the wish of this unselfish mother. He gave to those evil spirits the shapes that all men fear, the shapes of the alligator, the big snapping turtle, the gar fish with his rows of wicked teeth, and the snake known as the water moccasin. From that time the little Indian boys and girls could see those evil spirits and keep away from them.

WHY THE IRISES HOLD HANDS

THERE is a pretty blue and purple flower with a heart of gold which blooms in early spring in the swamps and along the streams of the gulf coast. It is called the blue flag or the wild iris. As long as it blooms it holds its head up as if looking for something. It seems to be waiting for something to happen. There is an old Indian legend that tells how this lovely flower came to be and why it lifts its head above the grasses around it.

There used to be along the coast of Texas a tribe of Indians who were more clever than any other Indian tribe had ever been. This tribe was an old one, and for many years the people had remembered what their fathers knew, and they taught the children all that the tribe had learned. Because of this the Indians knew how to do things no other tribes knew. They built large houses. They knew how to plant seeds in the soil and make them grow food. They knew how to paint on skins, carve bones and write the sign language.

Because these Indians were so clever the Great Spirit loved them very much. He would stretch himself out on a soft cloud high in the sky on summer days and look down on the Indians as they worked and played in their camp. Because he loved them he sent them gentle rains when their crops needed water. He made it easy for them to find birds and animals to eat. He answered their prayers.

But these Indians at last stopped praying. They began to forget about the Great Spirit who was so good to them, and to think they could do everything for themselves. They grew proud. They no longer looked toward the sky to talk with the Great Spirit, but began to look upon themselves as gods.

When the Great Spirit saw this he became very angry. He no longer loved the proud Indians. He decided to punish them. So it happened that while the people of the tribe were walking about their camp a great dark cloud came quickly over the sun in the blue sky, and the sky became black. Then the Great Spirit, who had sent the cloud, waited to see if this made the Indians afraid of him. They were not afraid, but went into their strong houses and laughed at the rain coming down. As the Great Spirit saw this he was more angry than ever. He decided to destroy the proud tribe.

He took a deep breath and blew strong winds across the Gulf of Mexico towards the camp. The clouds began to rush through the sky when he hurled them with his hands, and they hit each other and broke into sharp rain. He opened his mouth and shouted and out came thunder. Lightning darted from his angry eyes. Then the winds began to drive the waters of the gulf upon the land and into the camp of the Indians. Even now they were not afraid. They would not pray to the Great Spirit, though they saw the waves pounding into their camp and they knew the Great Spirit was making war against them. The water rose higher about their houses. At last they climbed to the roofs. Husbands and wives and children joined hands to die together. Still they did not cry out. Finally the rushing waters covered them all. Together they went down into the dark, rolling waves.

They were brave. As the Great Spirit saw this he thought that such people ought to have another chance to live. Perhaps they would become wiser and better if they lived again, so he decided that they would come alive when the last of the flood waters had rolled back into the Gulf.

While they waited to be brought to life once more they should have the form of a new kind of plant. The Great Spirit decided this. He turned them into plants as they lay under water, and because they were in the water they grew roots which could live in it and could live nowhere else. As they had died with their hands linked together they now took the form of plants with their roots linked together. When spring came the plants put forth blue flowers which lifted their heads to see if the last of the flood waters had rolled back into the Gulf so they could take the shape of people once more.

This is the way they grow to this day. We call them wild irises or flag lilies. They still grow in low and watery places. Their roots still cling together. Their heads are still lifted, for they are waiting to see when the last of the waters return to the Gulf. Each year they find the marshes and low places still filled with water and so they must wait a while longer.

And this is the legend of the wild iris.

THE PECAN TREE'S BEST FRIEND

IN almost every pecan grove in this part of the country you will find the little orchard oriole and his mate living and raising their families in the spring. Where you find pecan trees you will find this little black and chestnut fellow and his tiny yellow, green and brown wife. You see the trees and the orioles living together because once upon a time each did a favor for the other. The Indians remember.

One spring in the long ago an oriole family was living in its small nest of woven grasses swinging at the end of a branch on a tall pecan tree. The proud father bird and his wife were the parents of five little ones. As yet they could not fly, though their tiny feathers were beginning to grow large enough so that they could flutter to the edge of the nest and look over to see what the world looked like down on the ground. All day the parents gathered bugs for the little ones and sang their sweet songs. The big pecan tree liked the oriole family because they ate the bugs that tried to bore into the trunk or cut its leaves off. And so the tree and the birds got along like good neighbors

One day the father bird looked up and saw the sky beginning to fill with bits of white clouds like snow flakes and flying very fast towards the north. Soon he saw flying under the clouds those great wide-winged birds called frigate birds or men-of-war, which live far away on islands in the Gulf. These birds only fly inland when a hurricane, or storm, is getting ready to rush out of the Gulf of Mexico and blow its wild breath upon the coast country. The father oriole knew this. He knew by the clouds and the frigate birds that a storm was soon to strike the country where his little ones were waiting in the nest. He became frightened. When the pecan tree saw him fluttering around and around in distress the tree asked him what was the matter. The oriole told him that a storm was coming and would blow his five children away.

"I know what to do," said the pecan tree. "There is a hole under my biggest branch. Take your wife and babies into that hole and the wind will not touch you."

Thanking the good tree, the oriole father took his family into the hole and waited for the storm. They did not have to wait long. The next day the howling winds swooped into the grove with the black clouds and rain that came with the hurricane. All the trees bent their heads as ° the wind tore at their leaves. Branches were stripped from the tree, and the grass nest of the orioles was soon torn apart and scattered and carried away. But, safe in their hole, the oriole family listened to the wind howl and were glad that the pecan tree was good to them.

After the storm the father oriole decided he would do a good turn for the tree just as soon as he got a chance. He told the tree about this.

The pecan tree laughed and said, "What can you do for me, little bird?"

"Wait and see," said the oriole. "Something will give me a chance to help you."

He was right about that, too. One winter all the trees and bushes thought that the cold north wind would not come. Spring was about due, and the winter had been warm. The trees thought it was now too late for the north wind to make them a visit, and they began to put out their buds and leaves earlier than usual. One day down in Mexico, where the orioles always went during the winter months, the father oriole felt in his tiny bones that a cold spell was on the way from the north. He had heard that the trees in Texas were putting out their buds too soon. He knew that if his friend, the pecan tree, put out its buds the cold north wind would bring sleet and would freeze the buds, so that the tree could not have any pecans.

Here was a chance to do the pecan tree a good turn. The oriole flew quickly to Texas. He found his friend the pecan tree was about to put out its buds on the limbs.

"Keep in your buds and leaves!" cried the oriole. "A co d wind is on the way from the north and will hurt all the trees that are budding too soon." Then the oriole hurried back to Mexico before the cold weather could catch him.

The pecan tree laughed to itself and thought the oriole was wrong. But it decided it would wait until later to put out its buds. And how glad it was! For the next day the north wind made a late trip into the south, bringing the sleet and cold weather with it. It whooped and blew around the country, and all the trees and bushes had their early buds frozen off. All but the pecan tree who had been the friend of the little oriole, for this tree had not put out any buds. It was the only tree that bore pecans that year.

The other pecan trees learned about the good turn which the oriole had done for one of them. They became the friends of all orioles from that time, and this is why you find the little birds living and nesting wherever pecan trees are growing.

WHEN THE RAINBOW WAS TORN

THERE are flowers whose petals have in them part of the very colors belonging to the rainbow. These are the cactus flowers, the blooms which burst out like orange, red or yellow flame from the tips of the thorny cactus plants. It used to be that all these flowers were white, as some are now. But one day the rainbow gave most of them colors which they have kept up to this time.

The white cactus flowers used to turn up their faces and look at the bright bow that arched across the sky whenever the sun shone through the rain or mist. The two ends of the rainbow always touched the earth somewhere, and where they touched everything on the ground seemed to be washed in the rainbow's colors. But the rainbow had never touched the cactus plants. Perhaps it was afraid of the sharp thorns that grew on them. The white cactus flowers always hoped that some day they would be bathed in misty colors. Yet the rainbow would never come near them.

Once after a heavy rain the rainbow was up in the sky getting ready to send its two ends down to earth. The rainbow itself was heavy with raindrops. As its ends sank down it took care not to let them fall upon the thorns of the cactus plants. But, just as one of the ends was about to dip to the ground the rainbow suddenly saw a bed of cactus plants hidden in a little cluster of high grass. When it saw the plants the rainbow tried to lift its end again, but the end was so heavy with the raindrops that it kept sinking down, and at last it brushed across the cactus plants with their white flowers.

When this happened the thorns caught at the misty bands of colors to try to keep them for the flowers. The violet, indigo, blue and green bands slipped out of their way, but the yellow, red and orange bands became hung on the thorns. Just as soon as this happened the happy cactus flowers opened their petals wide and began to drink in the colored mists that were clinging to the plants. Before the rainbow had pulled itself loose from the thorns the white flowers had filled themselves with the colors and were now red and orange and yellow themselves.

PAISANO, HATER OF THE RATTLESNAKE

THERE is eternal war between Paisano and the rattles-nake. They are deadly enemies, but it was not always so. Once Paisano, who is the long-legged black and white bird called the road runner, or chaparral cock, was the rattlesnake's friend. But the two friends at last came to hate each other. This is the story of why they did.

The rattlesnake, like the great, highflying birds called the eagles, carried messages from the gods to the wise men among the Indians. He was given messages to carry because no animal dared to stop him on the way, for his bite was very dangerous. He was called Serpent With the Bells, because he had rattles on the end of his tail. When he shook his rattles and showed his sharp, poisonous fangs everything fled from his path, leaving him to go on with his message.

Now Paisano, the chaparral cock, wanted to carry messages from the gods also. With his long legs and his big feet he could run much faster than the rattlesnake, and when he grew tired of running he would open his black and white wings and fly a while. Paisano knew he could carry messages more quickly than the rattlesnake. All he wanted was a chance to show the gods how fast he was.

At last this chance came. Paisano was a curious bird, and he was always slipping silently around in the bushes and among the rocks. In this way he happened one day to hear the rattlesnake getting a message from the Great Spirit. It was a message to the wise man of an Indian tribe living far away. Paisano decided at once to carry the message himself, to show the Great Spirit how fast he was. He set out, running like the wind. Over the rocks and bushes he went, over the rivers and through the woods. His long legs moved so fast they seemed to twinkle. He ran till his tongue was hanging out, then he flew with a great flutter of his wings, and then he ran again. Paisano was in a hurry. Long before the rattlesnake had gone half the distance Paisano reached the camp of the Indians where lived the wise man who was to get the message of the Great Spirit.

Paisano gave him the message. He also told him how he had heard the Great Spirit talking to the rattlesnake. He begged the wise man to ask the Great Spirit to make him a message carrier because he ran so much faster than the rattlesnake could go. The wise man promised to help him.

When the Great Spirit heard about Paisano he decided to use the bird as a carrier of messages. But the Great Spirit did not like it because Paisano had listened when he was talking to the rattlesnake. For this reason he allowed Paisano to carry only little messages that didn't matter much. Even this did not please the snake. He was very angry with Paisano. He watched the nest where Paisano had his little ones, and when the bird was gone he went to it and swallowed all the little Paisanos. When the father bird learned what had happened he rushed away through the bushes and looked for the rattlesnake's little ones, and when he found them he ate them.

From that time began the war between Paisano, the chaparral cock, and the rattlesnake. Paisano stopped making his nest on the ground so the snake could not get his eggs and children. He began building his nest in bushes or in trees. Often he puts it among the thorny leaves of the cactus plant. Whenever he goes to his nest to carry food to his mate he first looks carefully around this way and that. He wants to be sure the rattlesnake isn't following him home.

MAIDENS WHO BROKE A DROUTH

FOR many days a tribe of Indians had suffered from a drouth that threatened never to end. The grass dried up. Berry bushes turned yellow and died as the hot sun kept burning down through the cloudless sky. The creeks ran dry and the fish died. Animals fled from the country because there was no more water to be found. Finally the Indians moved their camp and hunted for water, but nowhere could they find enough. Something had to be done. The chief of the tribe called on the medicine man to tell them what they could do to break the drouth and to bring down the rain once more.

Pointing to a high cliff the medicine man told the chief that a great serpent, the chief of all the snakes, had his den in a cave at the foot of the cliff. This serpent, said the medicine man, would have to be fed some of the maidens of the tribe. Then the gods would send down the rain.

As soon as they learned what the medicine man had said the young girls hurried to the chief and begged him to let them be thrown over the cliff to the chief of the snakes, so that their people could have the water they needed. All Indians were taught to be willing to give up their lives, if need be, for the sake of the tribe. Because they had been taught this the young Indian girls were not afraid to die, for they knew that their spirits would be taken up in the sky by their ancestors and honored for the good they had done their people. The chief was sad to lose the maidens of the tribe, but he thought the long drouth could be broken in no other way.

At last the girls who were to be thrown over the cliff to feed the chief of the snakes were chosen by lot and taken to the top of the cliff. The medicine man lined them up at the edge. They looked over and became dizzy when they saw how far it was to the bottom, where lay cruel rocks. But the maidens were brave. They waited for the medicine man to give them the signal to leap. When the medicine man had finished his dance and his prayers he raised his hand. Hand in hand the maidens jumped. Down, down, down they fell, their white robes fluttering. The parents of the girls turned their faces away, for they could not bear to see their daughters die.

But the brave Indian girls never died. They never dashed on the rocks. The goddess who watched over young girls was looking down from the sky and took pity on the maidens. Just before they reached the bottom of the cliff she turned them into white flowering bushes which took root on the spot. As the snake chief, who had been looking up and waiting with an open mouth for the maidens, saw this happen he was afraid, for he knew that some power greater than himself had been at work. He hurried back into his dark cave. As soon as he had gone the clouds which had been afraid to float over the land as long as the serpent was there now sailed back. Rain poured down from them and the long drouth was ended.

The bushes which had been the Indian maidens continued to grow and to spread in memory of the brave deed of long ago. We call these the bee brush or bush honeysuckle. They still grow in the canyons or gulches, all over central Texas and southward to the Rio Grande river. All summer they bloom and fill the air with fragrance. In the spring the plants are sought by hungry hummingbirds who sometimes nest in them. The bees come to gather honey from the flowers. Butterflies and moths hover over them. Perhaps these creatures know the story of the sweet-smelling bush.

WHY ARROWS HAVE FEATHERS

A baby hawk once fell from its nest in a high tree and lay on the ground, too young to fly. The little bird would have soon died from lack of food, or it would have been caught by an animal and eaten, if an Indian boy had not found it. The boy took the young hawk home with him and cared for the bird. He made it a nest on the top of a stump and fed the bird day after day until it at last was ready to fly, but the hawk did not leave. It liked the Indian boy who had saved its life. When the boy was playing around in the village the hawk sat on the stump where it had been raised and watched him.

One day the young Indian was making arrows from slim branches of trees and shooting them from his bow. At that time Indians did not put feathers on their arrows. Each time the boy shot an arrow it would fly straight for a little way and then turn over and over. The hawk saw this and had an idea. Why could not one of its wing feathers make an arrow fly straight?

The bird could not talk to the boy, but it pulled out a long feather and dropped it at the boy's feet upon one of the arrows that lay on the ground. The boy paid no attention to the feather. Then the hawk dropped another and whistled. So the young Indian saw that the hawk was trying to tell him something about the feathers. He picked up one that lay on the arrow at his feet, fastened it to the blunt end of the arrow and aimed at a tree far away. This time the arrow flew straight as the hawk. The Indians in the village gave a great shout, for at last they had found out how to make their arrows fly straight through the air.

THE COTTONWOOD REMEMBERS

WHEN April comes to stir the forests and fields into new life after the winter months have gone, the cottonwood tree spreads her arms and shakes her head and sends her white feathers floating down in the air. The cottonwood does this every year because she remembers something that happened long ago before the owl became a wicked bird who eats others.

In the beginning of things no bird killed another. All ate buds and leaves and grasses. The Great Spirit who made them, caused the birds to eat these things because he did not like to see anything that he had made killed by another creature.

The owl, at that long distant time, was not blind in the daylight, like he is now. He flew around with the other birds and fell in love with a white swan. She could swim. She liked to float on the waters of the river and to gaze at herself in the smooth water. But the owl was not made for swimming. He sat in a tree above the swan and wished he could be with her.

"Marry me, lovely swan," called out the owl one day as he watched her.

The white swan looked up at him and said, "Come down and we shall talk about it."

The owl was afraid of the water, but he was so much in love with the swan that he decided he would try it. So down, down he sailed from the limb. He struck the river with a splash. He tried to swim but he could not. He fluttered his wings and stirred up the water and scared the fish, but he could not swim. With his mouth full of water the owl at last rose from the river and flew up to the branch again. There he sat, dripping water and saying bad words.

"Ha, ha, ha!" came a laugh from the reeds along the river. The loon, a bird that swims under the water, had seen the owl try to swim and was laughing at him from behind the reeds. "Ha, ha, ha!" laughed the long-necked loon again. "The oldest fools are the biggest fools."

That made the wet owl angry. "Who, who, who?" he called out. He was full of rage, and his hooked beak snapped.

On the branch of the cottonwood tree on which the owl was sitting a wood pigeon was talking to her mate. The wood pigeons didn't know anything about the owl for they were busy talking. The husband asked, "Whom do you love?" Just as the owl cried out, "Who, who, who?" the pigeon's mate said to her husband, "You, you."

When the angry owl heard this he thought the pigeon was talking to him. Down he darted in a fury towards the limb on which the pigeons were sitting, and he struck the little pigeon with his strong claws and his heavy beak. He knocked some fluffy feathers from the poor pigeon as he caught her. The feathers floated down and brushed the cheek of the Great Spirit as he was walking by under the trees.

"What is this?" cried the Great Spirit. "Some bird is killed." He looked up at the cottonwood and saw the owl sitting on a limb with the little pigeon in one of his cruel claws.

"What has happened?" called out the Great Spirit.

The owl would not answer, but the loon laughed again and told about the owl and the swan and the pigeons.

Full of rage the Great Spirit decided to punish the owl. He waved his hand and the owl became blind when the sun was shining and the other birds were flying around. And so it happened that from that time the owl could not see except at night, when the other birds were hidden away from his cruel claws and beak. Now the owl flies only at night. He keeps calling "Who, who?" but nobody answers. The Great Spirit also punished the loon for laughing. He made the loon swim by himself on the rivers at night and laugh when the owl calls out.

The cottonwood tree remembers what happened that April day. Because she remembers how the little gray feathers of the pigeon floated down she always shakes out her own down. When the winds blew this through the forest and over the rivers the Indians used to say, "The spirit of the pigeon has come back to her husband."

WHY THE SKUNK WALKS ALONE

WHEN the Great Spirit made the first skunk he gave him fur spotted with black and white to help hide him from his enemies. If the skunk stood still in the shadows at night nothing could see him, and he was safe. But he was not satisfied. He was still afraid, and he asked the Great Spirit for something more.

This time the skunk was given sharper teeth and longer claws. Now he was a truly terrible little fellow. Nobody could see him in the dark, and nobody knew the skunk was around until he felt sharp teeth and long claws biting and scratching. The other creatures of the woods and prairie began to fear the skunk, the animal which wanders around looking for his food when the sun has gone to bed and the stars have come out.

But still the skunk complained. He wanted something more, something that would make everything run from him. This made the Great Spirit angry. He had done much for the little black and white animal, but the skunk was not satisfied. What the Great Spirit did now was to give the skunk a powerful smell. This smell was so strong that when the skunk's friends found out he had it they ran from him as quickly as his enemies did. That is why the skunk goes alone today. Dogs and birds and snakes and men all dislike his smell, and so they leave him by himself.

HOW THE TURKEY HID HER EGGS

THE big turkey cock is so proud of himself that he does not want his wife to pay attention to anything but him. He looks for her eggs when she lays, and if he can find them he breaks them with his beak. If the eggs have hatched he sometimes kills the little ones. There was a time, so says an Indian story, when the turkey's eggs were white. They could be easily seen. The turkey gobbler found so many of them that his wife decided to hide them.

She began hiding them under dead leaves and twigs in the woods. The old man turkey looked everywhere for the eggs, but they were nowhere to be seen, for they were lying under their little brown blankets. This made the turkey cock's wife happy. She kept on putting leaves on her white eggs, and often the dew fell and wet the brown leaves as they lay on the eggs. In time the dew washed some of the color from the leaves. It dripped upon the white eggs and spotted them.

So it came to pass that the turkey's eggs became spotted with brown. She no longer had to hide them, because they looked so much like dead leaves that old man turkey could not see them any more as he walked around in the woods.

WHY THE DOG'S EARS FLOP

IF you look at the kind of dog that sleeps on his master's front porch and begs for a bone at dinner and crawls away when his master shakes a stick at him you will see that this dog's ears do not stand up bravely. They flop. And his tail does not stand up, but hangs close to his legs. This dog acts as if he remembers something for which he is ashamed. Perhaps he does. A long time ago one of his ancestors did something that caused the race of dogs owned by the Indians to lose their pride.

Before the dog left his wild cousin the wolf and came out of the woods and off the prairies to live with man he was as wild as the wolf. His sharp ears stood straight up, always ready to warn him of an enemy so that he would be ready to fight. He held his tail high, for he was a free animal and full of pride. And he was afraid of no man.

One time the dog could find no food for many days, and he went close to the camp of a tribe of Indians to see if he could find something to eat there. He saw strips of deer and bear meat hanging on poles to dry. One of the Indians was turning the meat so that all parts of it would be dried by the sun. The hungry dog went to him and told the Indian that if he would give him a piece of the meat he would stay in the camp to live with the Indians and fight all other animals that came around the camp.

The Indian thought this was a good idea and he agreed to feed the dog. And so for the first time the dog became a friend of man. He fought off the bears and wildcats when they came too close. He helped the Indians when they hunted for rabbits. He barked at night if enemies came around. But the dog still held his ears straight and kept his tail proudly raised over his back, for he was not afraid of anything.

Then one night some of his wild cousins, the wolves, came to where the Indians lived. At first the dog growled and would not let them pass, but when they told him that they only wanted to see how he liked his new friends, the Indians, the dog stopped growling and began to talk with some of them. He didn't see the others sneak around his back and begin to steal meat that hung drying on the poles. At last they got all the meat. Then they laughed and ran off as fast as they could while the dog barked in anger.

But it was too late to bark now. The meat was gone. When the Indians woke and ran out of their wigwams they saw that the meat was gone and began to beat the poor dog and shout at him. He was so ashamed the wolves had fooled him that for the first time in his life his ears flopped down and his tail fell between his legs. He whined and crawled on his belly in the dirt. The poor dog looked so sorry that at last the Indians left him alone. But from that time on he lost his pride. He became afraid when men shouted at him and that is the way he remains today.

ABOUT THE TEJAS INDIANS

The White Man Finds the Tejas Indians

TEXAS is the largest state in this great land of ours. Long ago, long before Columbus came to the New World, the people who lived in Texas were not white. They had bronze-colored skins. They were called Indians, because the first white people who found them thought they had come to the far-off land of India.

In a number of ways the Indians of the New World were like us. We like to tell stories, and so did they. They did not write their stories on paper because they did not know what paper was, and so they learned their stories by heart and remembered them. Fathers and mothers told the stories to their children and the children told them again to their children when they had grown up.

The stories in this book came mostly through the Tejas Indians, who belonged to certain tribes of east Texas, but the Comanches, Alabamas, Wacos, Wichitas, Tonkewas, Attakapas, and Karankawas [1] gave us some of the stories. The peaceful Tejas Indians made treaties with the warlike tribes west of their country, such as the Comanches and Wacos. By doing this the Tejas people could go out of their own country to get the hides and meat of the buffaloes, which roved the western lands in great herds. Living between the Tejas tribes and the Comanches

---

[1] Wich´itas, Tom´kewas, Attak´apas, Karank´awas.

and other tribes of central and western Texas were the Wichitas, the Tonkewas and Attakapas. Along the gulf coast lived the Karankawas.

As we read the legends we shall find out what the Indians of long ago believed about the flowers that grew in the fields and the fish that swam in the rivers and the birds that sang and flew in the air. The Indians lived close to these things. They lived in the woods and on the open fields, gathered into villages. They knew how little animals lived in the bushes and trees. They walked under the trees and watched the animals eating and playing. At night they sat in their camps around their fires and heard owls hooting and wolves howling far away in the dark.

They watched the flowers grow by the rivers and in the woods and fields in the spring time. They knew where to find the pink azaleas, which grew on tall bushes. In the spring the woods were full of yellow jasmine flowers. Indian girls liked to pick these and tie them in their long black hair. Another flower which the Indians knew was the dogwood. This big white flower grew on trees. When the trees were in bloom the blossoms that covered them looked like large white butterflies resting on the green leaves. In the open marsh glades grew the purple gentians, and on the prairies the bluebonnets. Sometimes these flowers looked like purple ponds of water because there were so many of them growing together. When the wind blew across them their purple and blue heads moved like waves. The Indians liked these flowers and others which grew where they lived, and many of the legends in this book are about them.

The bronzed people who knew the animals and flowers and told stories about them were friendly. When the first white people came to east Texas from France and Spain they found that the Indians were good and peaceful, and so they called them Tejas

Indians, which means friendly Indians. The white men named the country the land of the Tejas. Today that land is called Texas because of this old Indian name.

The Tejas Indians were happy and friendly when the first white people came to their country more than two hundred years ago. It was a land of woods and fields. The only people who lived there were the Indians, and they did not live in big towns. They lived in villages. The villages did not have roads between them. When the Indians wanted to go from one to another they had to walk through the open fields or the forests, sometimes on narrow trails and sometimes without any trail at all.

When the white people came to the land of the Tejas the Indians were glad to see them. These white people came from Spain. Their leader was a soldier named Captain de Leon. He brought with him his soldiers, and also a good man named Father Massanet, who came to tell the Indians about the white man's God. When Captain de Leon came to the place where Father Massanet was later to build the first church in Texas the chief of the Indians met the white people. He could not speak their language, but he talked with them by making signs with his fingers. Captain de Leon gave the chief some clothes like those the white people were wearing, and this made the chief happy. He put them on and led the captain and his men to the Indian village. As they marched into the village they sang and waved their flags.

The Indians were glad to see the strange white people because the chief told them Captain de Leon was their friend. They always obeyed their chief. He ruled all the tribes of the Tejas Indians and the leaders of those tribes. When he needed to find out something he wanted to know or help in time of war he called the leaders of the tribes to his big grass-covered house. They all sat around the fire inside and talked about things with their chief. When they decided what to do the leaders would go home to their tribes and tell them what the chief had said.

Father Massanet soon set to work building the first church in Texas, named San Francisco de los Tejas. With the help of his priests he cut down trees and built the church out of logs. He had brought some bronze bells with him, and he put these on the little log church, which was in Cherokee county and near the Neches river. He started teaching the Indians. The Indians began learning the ways of the white people and the white people began to learn about the Indians. In this way the two races of people came together.

The white people began to come in great numbers. They killed the wild animals which the Indians had been eating and they took or bought the land where the Indians had their small farms. Now and then whites married Indian women, and in this way the blood of the Tejas people was mingled with the blood of the whites. Today only a small number of the pure-blooded Indians are left. Two tribes called the Coushattas and Alabamas in east Texas are not native to the state. A few Indians of other tribes live among the white people and work small farms and hunt for a living.

How the Indians Looked

The Indians had reddish-brown or bronze-colored skin. They stood tall and straight. They had strong arms and legs because they walked much when they were hunting or fishing or moving their camps from one place to another. Their hair was long and black. They did not cut it short, but let it grow long. Because they lived out of doors so much their eyes were bright and sharp. They could see little animals and birds moving high in the trees, far away on the hills and even in the twilight. Their ears were keen. They could hear small sounds like rabbits running in the grass, or birds singing high in the air over their heads, or deer calling to their mates in the woods.

How the Indians Dressed

In summer, when it was warm, the men wore only pieces of animal skin around their waists. In the winter they wrapped themselves in robes made of skins with fur on them or blankets which the women made. Indian women also wore skins and blankets. When the babies were still too little to walk their mothers carried them in sacks of skin tied to the mothers' backs. When the babies were in these sacks only their heads peeped out.

On their feet the Indians wore soft shoes made of skin. These shoes were called moccasins. They were soft because the skin had been beaten with rocks or chewed. Indians could walk through the woods in moccasins and not make a sound if they were careful not to step on dry sticks and break them. The Indians were always careful not to make noises while hunting or when engaged in wars with other tribes.

These people who lived in the land of the Tejas so long ago liked pretty things, as do most people everywhere. They liked bright colors. They sewed colored feathers on their clothes and on their blankets and tied them on their hunting bows. From the little redbird they got red feathers, blue feathers from the blue-jay, white ones from herons and geese, black ones from the crow and buzzard, yellow feathers from the oriole and meadow lark, and spotted feathers from the wild turkey, the prairie chicken, the hawk, and the eagle. Sometimes they could not find the colored feathers they wanted, and so they dyed white feathers with the juices of berries or roots. They liked to wear feathers in their hair. They would braid their long hair and stick two or three feathers in the braids. The chiefs of the tribes wore bonnets made of many feathers.

On their moccasins and clothes the Indians sewed little colored beads. They made these beads from many things. Some were made from red, black, yellow or blue clay rolled into balls. When the clay was still soft after they dug it from the earth they made holes in the balls by pushing little twigs through them. Then they heated the balls in fires. This made the beads hard. Today these beads are sometimes found on the banks of rivers or around the places where the Indians used to have their villages. Beads were also made from hard nuts and seeds. Sometimes the Indians made them out of the teeth of animals, and also out of the bones of animals and fish. When they could find soft stones they would make these stones into beads and cut pictures on them. Shells found in the rivers or at the seashore were made into beads by punching holes into parts of them. Parts of certain shells were used as money.

Indians used paint on their faces, arms and legs. They made their paint out of the juices of berries and also out of different colored clays by mixing the clay with water or with grease. They got this grease from animals. When they went to war the men put paint on their faces to make them look ugly so they could scare their enemies. When they danced in their villages they put red and yellow and white and black paint all over themselves and shouted and danced. We would not think they were very pretty, but they thought they were, and that made them happy.

Indian Homes

The Indians lived in strange houses. They did not have such things as bricks and the kind of wood with which we build houses now. When they could find young trees growing close together they bent them over until their tops were touching and then they tied the tops together. Most of the time they stuck poles into the ground in the shape of a circle and tied the poles together at the top. Around these poles they made the walls of their houses by tying thick branches from trees or bunches of grass. Their houses looked like round haystacks. They did not have any windows. The only way light could get into them was through the door; which could be closed by hanging skins over it, or through holes in the walls used to let out smoke from the fires.

Some of the Indians lived in tents. These Indians did not live long in one place, but moved around and followed the animals which they killed and used for meat. They made their tents by stretching skins over poles set up in the ground and tied together at the top. When the skins were stretched over the poles the tents looked like ice cream cones upside down. On the skins the Indians painted pictures of trees, the sun, animals, birds, fish and Indians fighting or playing. When a tribe got ready to move to a new place the Indians took the skins off the poles, and rolled up the poles in the skins. They carried the bundles with them when they went to a new camp. In this way they could move their villages without much trouble.

The Tejas people did not travel much. They had gardens. They could not move their gardens, so they stayed where these were. On the inside of their houses they did not have wood floors, but walked on mats made of grass or on blankets or skins laid on the bare earth. They slept on beds made by driving four short sticks into the ground like the legs of a bed. On these legs they tied vines and the soft branches of trees, then laid on top of these their skins and blankets. Their beds were quite soft.

There were not many things in their houses. They had no chairs or tables, but sat on the floor or on their beds. There were no lights. When night came they would lay wood on the fire inside the house and this would make a bright blaze. The Indians did not have any books to read, so they did not need lights very much. They did most of their work while sitting outside their houses during the daytime. Those who went away from their homes to work did so in gardens or fished or hunted. When night came they were tired, and went to bed early. On cold winter nights they piled wood on their fires to make a big, bright blaze to keep them warm while the winds blew and whistled high in the trees outside. They cooked some of their food on these fires.

How Food Was Cooked

The Indians cooked their food in several ways. One way was to boil things in jars or dishes made of clay. When an Indian woman wanted to make soup or boil meat or vegetables she put the food into one of these pottery dishes, poured water into it and set it on her fire until the food was cooked.

Sometimes the Indians cooked food in pottery that could not be put on fires without cracking. When they used this kind of pottery they boiled the water and food in the jar by dropping into it rocks which had first been heated in a fire. As soon as one rock had cooled it was taken out and another hot one put in its place. At last the water came to a boil. It was a slow way to cook, but the Indians had plenty of time.

Indians knew how to bake food, such as corn bread and beans. They baked these in ovens made of dried clay or mud into which they put burning wood or hot rocks. They baked some food, such as fish, by rolling the food in wet clay and covering it up in red hot ashes for a while.

They cooked their meat by cutting it into strips and smoking it over fires or by boiling it. They often did not cook it, but cut it into strips and hung it outside their houses in the sun on long poles until the sun had dried it. They dried their meat in the summer and ate it during the winter months when animals were hard to find.

Indian Pottery and Baskets

The Indians kept their food and water in dishes or bottles made of clay or in baskets of woven grass and branches from trees. The women made these things. When they needed a dish of clay they would go out to find the kind of clay they wanted on the banks of rivers or in fields where rains had washed away the soft dirt till the clay could be seen. This clay was mixed with water until it was soft and could be pressed into shape. The woman who was making the dish would roll it and pound it with her hands until it was the right shape and size. Sometimes she painted it with paint made from clay of another color. Sometimes she scratched pictures or lines on the dish when it was still soft. At last she put the dish into a fire and burned it and made it hard, so that it would hold water without leaking or falling to pieces.

These clay dishes and bottles are called pottery. They were made in many different shapes. Some were like bottles. These were used to hold water and berry juices. Others were like bowls. In them were kept the foods which the Indians raised in their gardens, and fruits, nuts and berries. They were all easy to break and had to be used with care. Many are to be found today in the places where the Indians had their villages. Sometimes they are broken into many pieces, but if all the pieces are found they can be glued together and made to look just as they were when the Indians used them many years ago.

Baskets which the Indian women made were often very pretty. Some were of long, tough grass. Others were of strips of bark or wood cut from trees. Baskets could also be woven out of vines and the long, slim branches of willow trees growing near the rivers and ponds. The baskets the Indians used looked very much like those which are made now. Some were painted with different colors. Some had beads and feathers on them, and handles made of strips of skin. In these baskets the Indians kept foods.

Indian Gardens, Fruits and Berries

The Tejas Indians had gardens and small farms from which they got part of their food. This was one of the reasons they did not roam far over the country as most Indians did. The women, not the men, did the work in these gardens. Men hunted and fished and fought battles and left the work in the villages to their women.

The Tejas people did not have big farms with fences around them. They planted only little pieces of ground because they did not have such things as ploughs. Most of the time two or three Indian women would work on the same garden together, and when the crops were ready everything was taken from the garden and put into one pile. From that pile each Indian took vegetables as these were needed by a family.

The land where they lived was very rich and would grow anything they wanted to plant in it. There was not much cold weather in the winter, so that their gardens were not killed by hard freezes. There was plenty of rain to make their seeds grow in the spring. They did not have to dig big rocks out of the ground because there were not many rocks where they lived.

They raised corn, beans, calabashes, berries, melons and pumpkins. Corn and beans could be kept and used in the winter by putting them away in baskets or jars. Peppers could be kept the same way.

In the woods the Indians found many things to eat. They knew where to find the wild pecan trees, the hickory nut trees and the walnut trees. They knew where vines with grapes grew. There were many kinds of berries growing wild, such as blackberries, dewberries, and huckleberries. Wild plum trees also grew in the woods. When the fruit and berries were ripe the Indian women and children would take baskets into the woods and go from tree to tree and from bush to bush until the baskets were full. Sometimes they were gone all day and did not go back to their camp before night began to fall in the woods. They liked the fruits and did not mind working hard to get them.

How They Hunted and Fished

Indians liked to hunt. It was fun to walk through the woods looking for rabbits or wild turkeys or to run after the deer and buffalo which roamed over the country. These Indian people had to hunt because it was the only way to get the meat they ate. Each father had to go out hunting meat for his own family. While the women stayed at home tending the gardens and keeping house the men spent much of their time going through the woods or across the open prairies with their bows and arrows.

The Indians used bows and arrows for shooting animals. The bow which the Indian used was much like the bows from which boys shoot arrows today. It was about five feet long and was made of the wood of different kinds of trees growing where the Indians lived. A cord made of skin was tied to each end of the bow and was pulled tight until the bow was bent. The arrows which were shot from the bow were also made of wood. An arrow had to be very straight so it would fly in a straight line. It had a point shaped from hard rock. Each tribe of Indians had a man who did nothing but make arrow points, because a man could not make these well unless he made many of them. The arrow maker would look on the ground for the kind of rock which he wanted. Then he would take another piece of rock and pound the first so that it was broken into flat, thin pieces shaped like leaves. From each of these pieces he would make an arrow point. He did this by chipping little bits off of them with a sharp stone until they had the right shape. Arrow points were both big and little. Indians used big ones on their arrows when they wanted to shoot large animals like deer or bears. When they wanted to shoot birds, such as wild turkeys, cranes and hawks, they used arrows with little points so as not to tear the birds to pieces.

Each hunter carried many arrows in a long leather sack which was called a quiver. He hung the quiver full of arrows over his shoulder so that he could quickly pull an arrow out of it when he wanted to shoot something.

A good hunter could hit an animal with an arrow when the animal was running fast, and he could hit birds as they flew in the air. All little Indian boys were taught how to use the bow and arrow just as soon as they were strong enough to hold them, and that is why Indians were such good hunters. Today the woods where the Indians hunted are full of arrow points. They can be found lying in ditches where the water has washed the dirt away from them. Sometimes one can be found sticking in a tree where the arrow hit when an Indian shot at an animal and missed it.

One of the animals which the Indians hunted was the buffalo, that once roamed in thousands over the plains. The buffalo was of great use to the Indians. They used his meat for food and his shaggy hide for making clothes, tents or blankets. Indians killed the buffaloes by driving them in large numbers into narrow paths between rocky walls until the animals came to high cliffs and fell over. Sometimes they drove them into rivers or muddy places and shot them with arrows. Another way to shoot the buffaloes was for the Indian hunters to dress themselves in buffalo hides to fool the animals and then creep up close enough to shoot arrows at them. After the white man came to America the Indians used horses for hunting. The Indians skinned the dead animals and carried parts of the meat back to their camps. When they had so much meat that they could not eat it all at once they cut it into thin strips, and hung it in the sun to dry. Dried meat lasted a long time.

In the woods the Indians hunted rabbits, squirrels, coons, turkeys and bears. They did not shoot animals just for fun. They only killed when they were hungry. Because of this the woods were always full of things which they needed for food. On still summer days they could hear the big turkey gobblers calling to their flocks. They could hear squirrels barking and scolding one another up in the oak trees. If they stood still and hid themselves they could see the little rabbits hopping along in the grass and nibbling leaves. They knew where to find the tracks which the little black coon made in soft mud with his paws on the banks of rivers when he came to drink at night or to catch crawfish in the water. They knew where the big bear had been walking when they saw his footprints looking like the hand of a giant in the dirt. At night when they heard something howling on the plains they knew it was a wolf.

The best hunters could call animals and birds to them. They could whistle like the larks and bob-whites. They could call the wild turkeys close to them. They could bark and scold like the squirrels. Hunters who could do these things did not have to walk, but stood still in the woods and called the animals close enough to shoot them.

How They Got Food from the Water

The Indians also fished. They got part of their food from the rivers and lakes, which were full of fish of many kinds. They caught them with hooks and lines. They made hooks out of thin rock and bones, much as they made their arrow-points. It was hard work to make hooks, and they were easy to break. The hooks were tied on lines made of long strips of skin, sinews, long vines or hair. On these hooks and lines the fishermen caught the large fish, such as the catfish, the gar, the buffalo fish and the drum. Once in a while they would catch a big turtle, but the Indians got most of their turtles by digging them out of the ground after the turtles had buried themselves for the winter.

Sometimes the Indians shot fish with their bows and arrows. They would stand very still near the river and wait until a fish swam close to the top of the water, then shoot it with an arrow and catch it before it could float away. The fishermen also used nets made of vines. They would drag them through the water and catch the big fish in them, or would put food in the nets and leave them in the water where fish would become caught in them.

Indians liked to eat clams, and these were easy to get. They waded in rivers and picked up the clams lying on the bottom. Some clams buried themselves in mud or sand in the rivers. The Indians found these by digging with their feet or hands where they knew the clams were hiding. Indians who lived near the waters of the Gulf of Mexico waded into the shallow water near the shores and found many oysters, which taste somewhat like clams.

The Gods of the Indians

The people of the Tejas country believed in many spirits. They thought some of these were good and that others were bad. Everywhere, they believed, the spirits were watching them. When a storm arose and howled through the trees it was evil spirits wailing and shouting. When leaves rustled and whispered in the tops of trees in summer it was good spirits talking among themselves or playing together. Spirits caused the lightning to shoot across the sky, made water bubble out of the ground, caused the snow to fall and ice to form on ponds of water, turned the leaves red and yellow when winter came, made the flowers bloom in the spring and caused fire to leap and dance.

Each Indian tribe had what was called a medicine man, who was able to talk with these spirits. The medicine man believed that he could talk with spirits who lived in the woods and sky, and he told the Indians what the spirits were doing and what they said.

There were the evil spirits, which the Indians feared. There were also the good spirits, which helped the Indians. The medicine man thought he knew how to keep the bad spirits from hurting the Indians and how to get the good spirits to give them what they wanted. He kept a fire burning night and day in the big house where he lived. From it all the Indians got burning bits of wood which they took to their homes to build their own fires with, because they thought the medicine man's fire had magic in it. The medicine man did not have to work like other people of the tribe. Indians brought him fish and birds and other things to eat, and the women cooked for him and made his clothes. Even the chief thought he was a very wise man.

The medicine man helped the great chief of the Indian tribes. When the chief wanted to know something which nobody else could tell him he went to the house of the medicine man. He asked the wise man things about hunting or where to find water, or how to make the rain stop, or how to cure sick people. Then the medicine man painted his body with bright colors and put a cap of feathers on his head. Sometimes he would shout and dance until he was so tired he fell to the ground. He often swallowed a magic drink which he had made, and this drink would make him say strange things, and the Indians thought he was talking with the spirits. After that he would tell the chief what he wanted to know.

The medicine man was many times wrong, but the Indians did not remember when he was wrong, and they always remembered it when he was right. Because of this they thought he was a very wise man with magic powers. When they wanted to go to war they asked him how they should begin and where they should fight. When they needed rain for their crops they asked him to pray for the spirits to send it down from the sky. When the hot sun burned from the sky for day after day they asked him to pray to the spirits to send clouds to make it cool and make the rain fall.

Sometimes, the Indians thought, an evil spirit would get into a man and make him sick or crazy. They had ways to drive out this evil spirit. The medicine man of the tribe would make medicine out of different things and give it to the man, or he would put seeds, hair, bones and other things into little bags called charms and tie these about the man's neck to drive out the evil spirits. If many people of the tribe got sick the other Indians would dance and shout and pound on drums to make a great noise so that the evil spirits which caused the people to be sick would become scared and would go away from the camp.

When the people wanted the good spirits to give them something they often danced and sang and prayed in their camps so the spirits would hear them and be pleased. They would paint their faces and put flowers and feathers in their hair. The medicine man would make magic drinks and swallow them so he could talk better with the spirits. Then everybody would begin to dance. Sometimes they danced all day and all night. The weaker Indians would soon fall to the ground, but the others kept on leaping around and shouting their songs to the sky, where they thought the spirits were watching and listening. When night came some of the Indians piled logs on the campfires. The bright flames roared and climbed high in the air and made the camp as light as day. The dogs barked, the Indian children laughed and the dancers sang as loud as they could. At last the Indians were so tired they fell to the ground and slept there or crawled to their houses and went to bed. Sometimes the spirits gave them what they wanted. At other times they did not, for the good spirits did not always hear the Indians, so the medicine man said.

The Indians had a god they called the Great Spirit, who ruled all the other spirits, both good and bad. He lived somewhere up in the sky, where he could see all things that happened on the earth. He knew when a baby died. He saw every wolf on the prairie. He knew when it was going to rain, when a storm was about to come, when an Indian was going to get hurt and when a little ant fell off a leaf in the woods. He knew these things because he ruled everything on the earth and nothing could happen unless he wanted it to happen.

The people of the Tejas country believed that when they died the Giver of Life took them to heaven, where they lived just as they had done on this earth but did not have the troubles they had here. They believed that they needed their bows and arrows for hunting up there in the sky. They thought that after they died they would need everything they used on the earth. Because of this they buried their people with all the things used and loved when they were alive. When a hunter died his family would put in the grave with him his clothes, his bow and arrows and his knife. When a little child died they would bury it with dolls or other things it liked to play with. When an Indian woman died they would bury her with her pretty clothes, beads, moccasins, necklaces and bone needles.

The Indians loved and worshipped the Great Spirit or Giver of Life. Some of the legends in this book tell how the Great Spirit brought help to the Indians when they were in trouble. The legend named "Why the Irises Hold Hands," tells how the Great Spirit grew angry and sent a flood upon some Indians who did not thank him for the good things he had given them. In the legend called "Kachina Brings the Spring" it is told how the Great Spirit sent down rain to the Indians after a little girl had burned her doll to please him.

We have seen how the Indians lived close to the animals and fish and birds and how much they knew about these little things that ran, swam and flew. We have found that the Indians believed in good and evil spirits and a Great Spirit who was most powerful of all. Now we know why the legends in this book tell us about these things. The Indians thought about them all the time, and because of that they put them into their stories. The legends tell us what the Indians thought about the world in which they lived.

INTERESTING THINGS TO DO

1. Make an Indian book showing:

types of Indian homes

the dress of several tribes

designs on Indian pottery

designs on Indian baskets

designs on Indian blankets

An encyclopedia will give you some of the information you need.

2. Make some designs of your own for pottery, baskets, or blankets. Use the Indian symbols given in the book and combine them in different ways.

3. List all the things that you have found out about the Tejas Indians.

4. Choose a story to dramatize. Some are more easily dramatized than others.

5. Find the names of some plants from which the Indians made dyes. Get some herbs, roots, and flowers with which you can make dye. Dip various kinds of material in these dyes and see which materials take dye the best.

6. Find out:

In what kind of place the mescal plant grows.

Whether orioles nest in the pecan trees.

If there are many birds on the islands off the coast of Texas.

If there is a little brown center in the magnolia blossom.

If the flowers of the wild orchid point south.

Is the Spanish moss helpful or harmful to trees? For what is it used?

7. Compare the actual nature facts with the things that the Indians believed about the following:

Why does the woodpecker peck the trees?

Why do owls see better in the night than in the daytime?

What causes hurricanes?

What causes the rainbow?

What makes the clouds?

Why does the mistletoe grow in trees?

What are the "amber tears" of the sweet gum tree?

8. In many different countries there are myths and legends that are much alike. How do you suppose this came to be?

Compare the Greek myth of Pandora with the story How Sickness Entered the World.

Compare the two legends of the magnolia given in this book. They were told by different Indian tribes. Which one do you like the better?

Compare the story Why Hummingbirds Drink Only Dew with the fable of The Hare and the Tortoise.

9. Find other stories about the rainbow.

INDIAN SYMBOLS

THE Indians used signs or symbols to represent words. There were many of these signs; only a few are shown on the following pages. These are the symbols that the artist used in making the colored pictures.

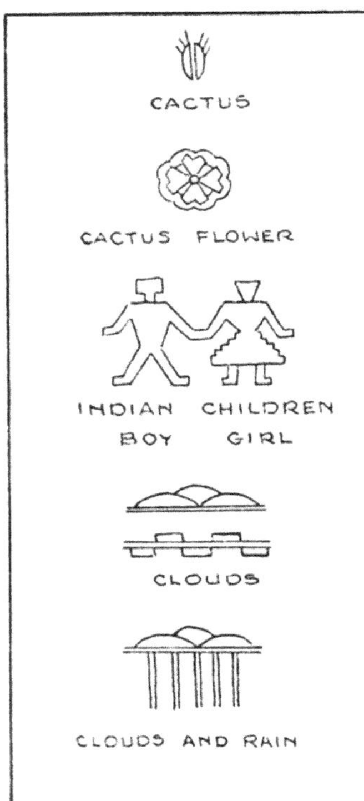

CACTUS

CACTUS FLOWER

INDIAN CHILDREN
BOY   GIRL

CLOUDS

CLOUDS AND RAIN

COMBAT OF
NORTH AND SOUTH WIND

DOG

EVENING STAR

FEATHER

FISH

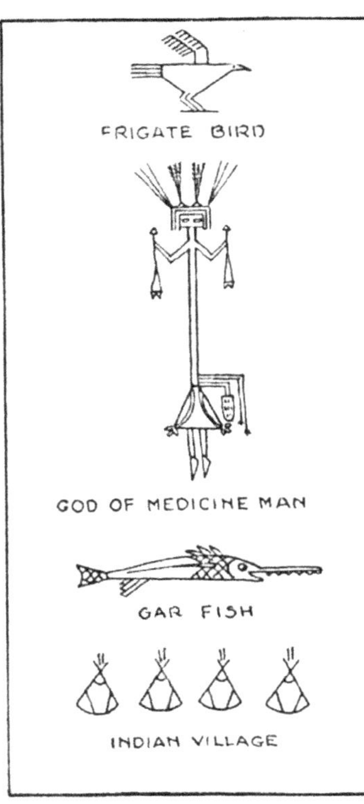

FRIGATE BIRD

GOD OF MEDICINE MAN

GAR FISH

INDIAN VILLAGE

IRIS

ISLANDS

KACHINA — INDIAN DOLL

LILY PADS ON WATER

LAKE SHORE

MAGNOLIA BUDS AND FLOWER

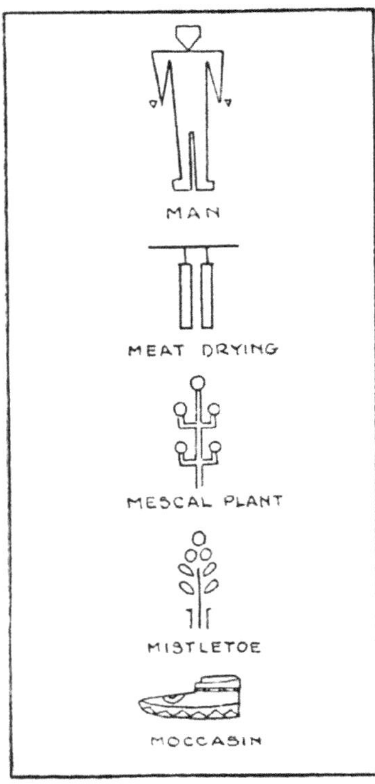

MAN
MEAT DRYING
MESCAL PLANT
MISTLETOE
MOCCASIN

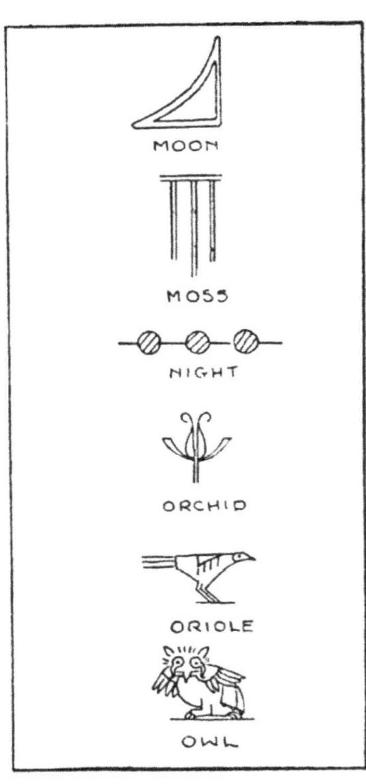

MOON
MOSS
NIGHT
ORCHID
ORIOLE
OWL

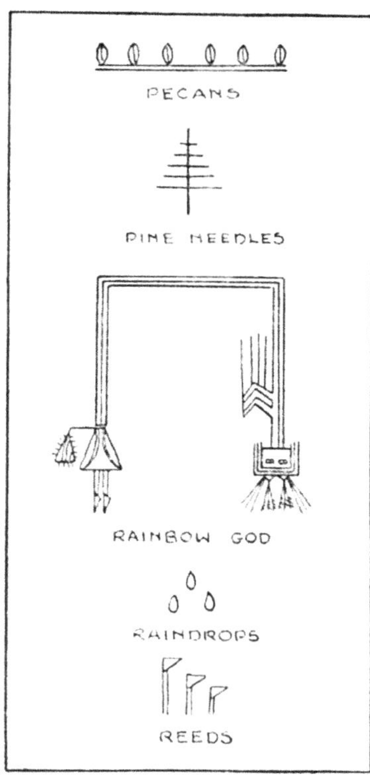

PECANS
PINE NEEDLES
RAINBOW GOD
RAINDROPS
REEDS

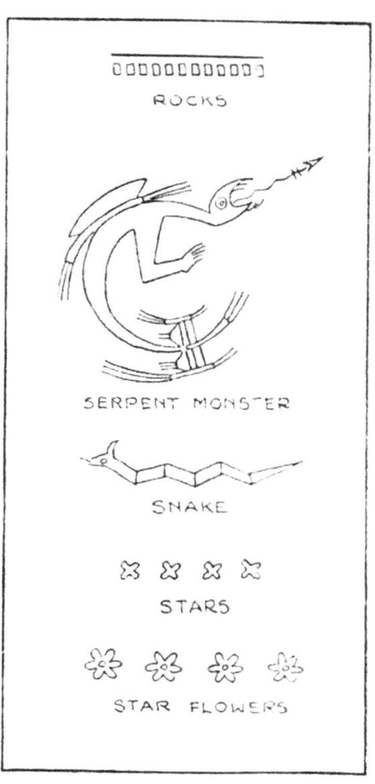

ROCKS
SERPENT MONSTER
SNAKE
STARS
STAR FLOWERS

WARRIOR
WATER
WEEDS
WILD PHLOX
WOLF
WOMAN
WOODPECKER

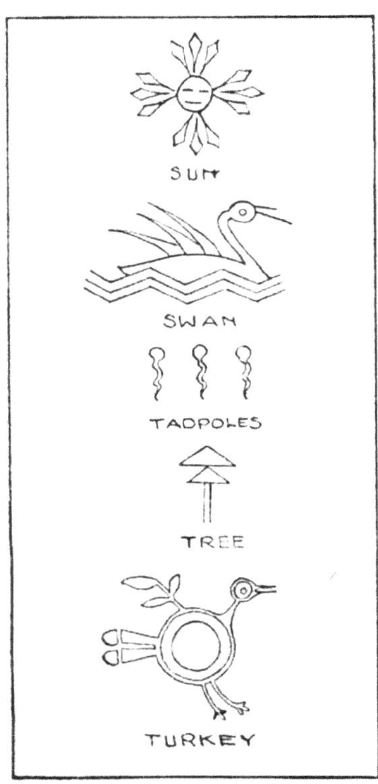

SUN
SWAN
TADPOLES
TREE
TURKEY

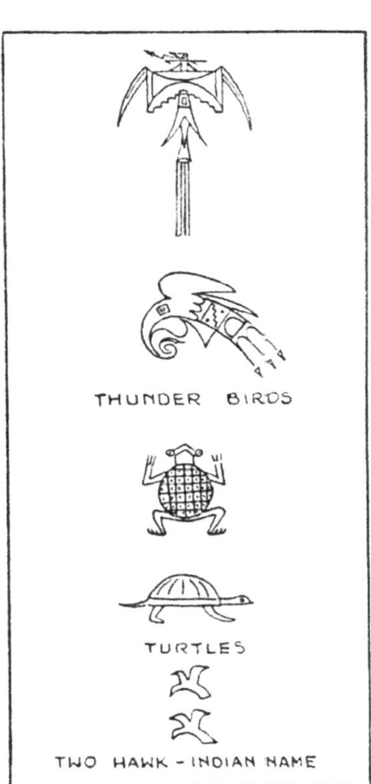

THUNDER BIRDS
TURTLES
TWO HAWK - INDIAN NAME